"I'm going down," Jack said.

He had done it before, although not with favorable results.

Pulling rope off his pack, he anchored it to a nearby tree root jutting out from the mountain. Romeo shot him a look, like, *Don't go without me.*

"Stay," Jack said in case the dog got any crazy ideas and shouldered his pack, which had supplies.

Gripping the rope with gloved hands, he let himself drift so he'd land gently on the plateau, about a hundred feet down.

He wouldn't be too late this time, wouldn't let any harm come to the woman in the blue ski jacket.

A few moments later he landed on the small ledge.

Her back was to him and she acted as if she hadn't heard his landing. "Miss?"

Startled, she turned suddenly, her eyes wide with fear. "Don't hurt me!" She stepped back, precariously close to the edge.

He instinctively reached out to grab her arm.

"No, don't!"

She stumbled backward over the edge of the cliff.

An eternal optimist, **Hope White** was born and raised in the Midwest. She and her college sweetheart have been married for thirty years and are blessed with two wonderful sons, two feisty cats and a bossy border collie. When not dreaming up inspirational tales, Hope enjoys hiking, sipping tea with friends and going to the movies. She loves to hear from readers, who can contact her at hopewhiteauthor@gmail.com.

Books by Hope White

Love Inspired Suspense

Hidden in Shadows
Witness on the Run
Christmas Haven
Small Town Protector
Safe Harbor
Baby on the Run
Nanny Witness
Mountain Hostage

Echo Mountain

Mountain Rescue
Covert Christmas
Payback
Christmas Undercover
Witness Pursuit
Mountain Ambush

Visit the Author Profile page at Harlequin.com.

MOUNTAIN HOSTAGE

HOPE WHITE

LOVE INSPIRED SUSPENSE
INSPIRATIONAL ROMANCE

LOVE INSPIRED® SUSPENSE
INSPIRATIONAL ROMANCE

ISBN-13: 978-1-335-72149-5

Recycling programs for this product may not exist in your area.

Mountain Hostage

Copyright © 2020 by Pat White

This edition published by arrangement with Harlequin Books S.A.

For questions and comments about the quality of this book, please contact us at CustomerService@Harlequin.com.

Love Inspired
22 Adelaide St. West, 40th Floor
Toronto, Ontario M5H 4E3, Canada
www.Harlequin.com

Printed in U.S.A.

Now the God of hope fill you with all joy and peace
in believing, that ye may abound in hope,
through the power of the Holy Ghost.
–Romans 15:13

To the volunteers of King County Search Dogs, State of Washington, for their commitment to saving lives.

ONE

Zoe Pratt lost her footing on the icy trail and gasped. Stabbing her hiking stick into the snow for balance, she peered over the steep drop below into the vast, white blur of nothingness. A shudder ran down her spine.

Maybe a winter hike hadn't been the best idea.

"Shannon, slow down!" Zoe called, recentering herself to keep up with her friend.

"I can't," Shannon said. "Wait till you see the view from Prairie's Peak!"

"Do we have to risk our lives getting there?"

"You know I'd never let anything happen to you."

Zoe adjusted her red scarf to cover her mouth and nose. It was cold in the Cascade Mountains, and Zoe wasn't an experienced hiker. She'd come to the charming town of Mt. Stevens, Washington, to hang out with Shannon, her childhood best friend. Zoe thought they'd spend time relaxing, catching up on their lives, maybe even laughing a little. She eyed the steep drop to her right. Nothing to laugh about there. One wrong step and—

"Pick it up, pokey!" Shannon teased.

Zoe glanced at the gray sky. Light snow began to fall. "You sure it's safe out here?"

"What, you're not afraid of a grizzly, are ya?"

"A grizzly as in a bear?"

"They're probably more afraid of you than you are of them." Shannon continued her enthusiastic pace and Zoe struggled to keep up.

Shannon had always been the one to challenge Zoe out of her funk when things seemed desperate. Well, things weren't exactly desperate, but Zoe did need a break, both from her challenging job as a social worker for adolescents and teens, and from her dismal personal life. She still couldn't believe how badly she'd misjudged things with her ex-boyfriend, Tim.

Shove it aside, Zoe. This was supposed to be a rejuvenating getaway, not a depressing one.

Zoe inhaled the fresh mountain air and let it clear her lungs, her thoughts. She felt grounded and at peace in the mountains. She could see why Shannon loved it so much and why she thought it the perfect place to bring Zoe.

She caught up to her friend, who hesitated at a small outlook, gazing out across the Cascade mountain range.

Shannon eyed Zoe's jacket. "You warm enough?"

"Sure, I'm okay."

"Yeah, you should've worn my spare, matching jacket."

"And look like a pumpkin?" Zoe eyed Shannon up and down.

Shannon smiled, then redirected her attention to the horizon.

Zoe noticed a tower in the distance. "What's that?"

"Portage Fire Lookout. It's ridiculously easy to get to from the Frontage trailhead. You can really see the vastness of God's beauty from that spot." She glanced at Zoe. "It helps to get perspective on things."

Zoe smiled. "This is exactly what I needed to get my mind off my love life."

"Yeah, tell me about it."

"Are you having problems with Randy?"

"Who knows."

Zoe had noticed a photo of Randy and Shannon tucked in a kitchen drawer as if it had been recently put away, out of sight. The couple looked happy, both with wide grins, although Randy's was partially hidden by a full beard.

"Shannon?" Zoe prompted.

"He's been acting weird lately and I haven't heard from him since he left a few days ago to visit family in Denver."

"I'm sorry."

"No." She touched Zoe's shoulder. "We're not going to let guy trouble spoil our fun. Come on."

"How much farther?" Zoe asked.

"Depends how slow you hike." Shannon winked. "Race ya?"

"Ah, come on, Shan. What are you trying to do, prove how out of shape I am?"

"You'll thank me later when you sleep like a

baby." Shannon picked up her pace. "I packed snickerdoodles for our snack. That should motivate you."

"With red and green sprinkles?"

"Of course!"

Before Zoe could open her mouth to demand a snickerdoodle for sustenance, Shan had reached a sharp turn up ahead and was out of sight.

It made sense that Shan could outhike Zoe, considering Shan's job at the Mt. Stevens Resort was mostly physical, whereas Zoe's job required hours of sitting and listening.

A woman's scream echoed across the mountain.

"Shannon!" Zoe called.

Adrenaline coursing through her body, she rushed to get to her friend. She must have twisted an ankle or injured herself somehow. "Shannon, answer me!"

Nearly losing her footing, she took a deep breath. *Slow me down, Lord. Keep me safe.* If Zoe injured herself as well, she'd be no help to Shannon.

As Zoe reached the turn, Shannon darted around the corner and slammed into her. "Run, Zoe, run!" She pushed her for encouragement.

A bear, it had to be a bear, right? There was no way they could outrun a bear. Zoe had seen her share of National Geographic specials on wildlife. Would he try to eat them or—

"Stop!" a male voice said.

That didn't sound a like a bear.

"Don't stop, Zoe!" Shannon said.

Zoe focused on bending her knees to give her balance as she scrambled down the trail. Her pepper spray, why had she left it back at the house? *Because you didn't expect to need it out here*, she told herself. She thought hikers were nice sorts of people, nature lovers, tree huggers and— Shannon slammed into Zoe from behind. Zoe slid and prayed. *Please, Lord, not now, I'm not ready to end my work on earth!*

With a thunk, she hit a boulder meant to guard hikers at the outlook from the steep drop below. She glanced up…

In time to see a man the size of a pro wrestler grab Shannon from behind.

"No! Let go of me!" Shannon cried, trying to pull away from him.

The guy, wearing a brown snow jacket and maroon ski mask, started dragging her away.

"Zoe, run!"

Instead, Zoe scrambled to her feet and went after them. *Pay attention, Zoe. Pay attention to every detail.* They were going to survive this assault and she would have to testify against this creep.

She grabbed Shannon's arm and swung at the guy with her hiking stick. With a frustrated grunt, he threw Shannon aside and yanked on Zoe's stick, pulling her within inches of his face.

Those eyes. She'd never forget his practically black eyes, glaring at her from behind the knit mask.

"This is not your fight," he said in a low, threatening voice.

"She's my best friend!" Zoe struggled to pull free.

"Then you'll die with her."

"Leave her alone!" Shannon charged and hit the guy shoulder to midsection. A linebacker couldn't defend himself against her velocity, a skill Shan had learned from her two football-playing brothers.

The attacker loosened his grip and Zoe wrenched free from his hold.

"Run, Zoe!"

The man grabbed Shannon again, and she struggled against him. He started to hoist her over his shoulder, but she managed to rip off his ski mask.

His long, angular face, flushed bright red with anger, etched itself in Zoe's brain. He was in his midthirties with a scar above his left eye.

"Let me go!" Shannon cried.

Zoe charged, more out of instinct than intellect, and in one swift motion, the giant backhanded her.

Zoe's head snapped to the side and she stumbled back over the edge…

…into the white abyss below.

* * *

The text came in at 1:21 p.m.

Search-and-rescue volunteer Jack Monroe subtly flashed the alert on his phone to his second-in-command, Heather Bond, and excused himself from the business meeting with Brighton International. This was why he'd hired Heather: to manage his IT security business so he'd have the flexibility to leave Seattle and join a search when necessary. Depending on the mission he could be gone for days, taking up temporary residence close to the action.

At 3:02 p.m., Jack pulled up at the command center in the Cascade Mountains with Romeo, his border collie–Bernese mix, and was given instructions by the command chief.

By 3:15 p.m., Jack and Romeo had joined a team and were hiking up Mt. Stevens. Their assignment: find a fallen and suspected injured hiker, called in by a pair of hikers who had heard a woman scream and seen someone in a royal blue jacket fall down the mountainside. They weren't sure where she'd landed.

Fresh snow covered the trails and the wind was picking up.

"Amateur hikers should never go out in this kind of weather," Beatrice Spears said under her breath. Bea's Lab mix, Cooper, continued his search for scent.

"It was supposed to be mild in the mountains

today," Leslie Vonn said. Her dog hadn't been qualified yet, but it was good to have the extra person to offer praise when the dogs found the lost hiker.

When. Because *if* was not an option in Jack's mind.

"Did you hear about the hiker who disappeared at Crystal Mountain last weekend?" Bea asked.

"Got buried in an avalanche?" Leslie recalled.

"The dogs found her in less than twenty minutes. Fast."

Jack listened. He wasn't much for small talk, didn't know how to execute it effectively or, for that matter, what the purpose was. Another reason he'd hired Heather.

"I think Cooper's got something," Bea said.

The three humans watched Cooper zigzag up ahead. Something sparked in Jack's chest, a familiar pang whenever one of the dogs caught scent and went into a hyperfocused state.

Maybe this would be an easy rescue, unlike…

Hope dissolved into frustration as the memory surfaced. He shoved it aside. There was no added value in remembering his failure.

Romeo raced ahead of Cooper and stopped, nose in the air, tail up, intently focused. The team caught up to Romeo on the snow-covered trail, where the dog stood over a red scarf. Jack praised him for the find, then Romeo sat, awaiting further instruction.

"Think it belongs to the victim?" Bea said.

"It's possible." Leslie reported their finding to Command. "Let's continue up the trail."

"If the victim was seen falling from the Prairie's Peak area, how would her scarf end up here?" Bea said.

"Maybe it's not hers," Leslie said.

"Or she was coming down the trail when she fell," Jack finally said.

The women glanced at him, as if they'd forgotten he was there. Jack liked it that way, dissolving into the background, watching, listening, so he could better understand people.

Another twenty-one minutes passed as they continued their ascent. The snow had let up a bit. Jack naturally hiked ahead of the women due to his tall stature and long gait.

They had gone silent, probably not wanting to interrupt the dogs' focus, especially now that they knew they were on the right track. Another reason Jack liked being part of this group was the singular concentration required by the work. The ability to multitask mystified him as much as small talk. When he directed his attention to something, it became his sole focus.

Like today's mission.

"It'll be dark soon," Leslie said.

Her words hung in the cold air between them. Although the team was skilled at making camp overnight, the woman who'd fallen and was potentially injured would be ill-prepared for the drop in temperature.

Romeo started a zigzag pattern, then abruptly stopped. His ears pricked.

Jack took a deep breath. Suspected what was coming.

Romeo took off into a full sprint, and Jack followed, frigid air filling his lungs. It was senseless to tell Romeo to slow down. Once the dog caught scent, nothing would stop him. It made him an excellent search-and-rescue dog, but sometimes his enthusiasm made Jack nervous. He feared the hardworking dog might lose his footing and slide off the edge.

Jack pushed harder to catch up to Romeo. The dog was trained to return to Jack's side and pull on his toggle if he found something. Back and forth, back and forth, until Romeo united his handler with the missing hiker. Instead of exhibiting his trained indication, Romeo frantically paced at the edge of the trail up ahead. Jack interpreted this as him being in scent, but unable to make physical contact with the subject. Cooper ran up to Romeo and exhibited similar behavior.

Jack approached the dogs and glanced at what sparked their excitement.

A person in a royal blue jacket lay on a plateau.

"Good boy, good." Jack played a quick game of tug-of-war with Romeo as his reward as he radioed Command. "I think we found her, over."

"Status?"

He peered over the edge, sensing Bea and Leslie come up on either side of him. "Miss?" Jack called down to the prone hiker. "We're with Mt. Stevens Search and Rescue!"

Silence.

"Unresponsive, over," he said into his radio.

"Location?"

Jack opened his tracker app, took a screenshot and texted it to Command.

"We'll send a medical team," the command chief responded.

"Roger, out."

The search-and-rescue K9 team hovered on the trail in stoic silence.

"You think she's alive?" Bea asked.

Leslie glanced up at the mountain. "Depends on how far she fell. If she hit anything…" she hesitated "…critical."

More silence.

"I'm thinking this is a recovery, not a rescue," Bea said.

"Miss? Miss, can you hear me?" Jack shouted, not liking the direction of the conversation.

Romeo barked as if he was also trying to get her attention.

Jack hated this, hated feeling…out of control of a situation.

Romeo must have felt the same way, because

his barking grew more insistent as if he were saying, *Open your eyes already!*

"Romeo, stop," Jack commanded. The dog quieted and flopped down beside him.

Jack glanced at the horizon, realizing they had less than ninety minutes before they lost natural light. Rescuing the woman in the dark would present its own set of challenges.

"Wait, I think she's moving," Leslie said.

He snapped his gaze to the plateau. The victim started to get up.

Jack whipped out his binoculars. Peered below. He had to try to get a read on her expression even though that wasn't his particular strength.

A bruise formed across her right cheek and blood seeped from her lip. Her eyes rounded with fear as if she suddenly realized she was in a vulnerable, dangerous spot.

"Don't move!" he called. "I'm with Mt. Stevens Search and Rescue!"

She acted as if she didn't hear him, as if she were disoriented beyond rational thought, which meant she could accidentally fall even farther...

To her death.

"Medics are on the way!" he tried.

Ignoring him, she dropped to her knees and glanced over the edge of the plateau. What on earth was she doing? It seemed like she was trying to figure out how to climb down. A decision that was both unrealistic and potentially deadly.

Then again, she could be dazed from a concussion and not know what she was doing.

"I'm going down," Jack said.

"Wait, shouldn't you—"

"He's right," Leslie interrupted Bea's protest. "Who knows what she'll do? Besides, Jack's done this before."

He had done it before, although not with favorable results.

Pulling rope off his pack, he anchored it to a nearby tree root jutting out from the mountain. Romeo shot him a look, like, *Don't go without me*.

"Stay," Jack said, in case the dog got any crazy ideas. He shouldered his pack, gripped the rope with gloved hands and let himself drift so he'd land gently on the plateau, about a hundred feet down.

He wouldn't be too late this time, wouldn't let any harm come to the woman in the blue ski jacket.

A few moments later he landed on the small ledge. Her back was to him and she acted as if she hadn't heard his landing. "Miss?"

Startled, she turned quickly, her eyes wide with fear. "Don't touch me!" She stepped back, precariously close to the edge.

He instinctively reached out to grab her arm.

"No, don't—" She stumbled backward over the edge of the cliff.

TWO

Jack dove and caught the woman's arm. It wasn't too hard, considering she waved both of them like a helicopter trying to take off, or in her case, a woman trying to stop the momentum that would catapult her down a mountainside.

He landed on his chest, and air rushed from his lungs, but he didn't let go. He grabbed her arm with his other hand, as well. Considering his size versus the petite victim's, he calculated a more than 50 percent chance of hoisting her safely up.

"Don't! Don't hurt me!" she cried, thrashing about.

If she kept squirming, his chances dropped way below 50 percent. "Stop moving or I won't be able to pull you up."

"Why, so you can kill me?"

Kill her? At this point he had to assume she'd hit her head and was suffering from delirium. At the very least she was irrational, which meant she was unpredictable and potentially dangerous. Especially if she kept shifting and broke free of Jack's grip, or even pulled him over the edge with her.

Jack scanned his brain for information on overly excited people and how to manage them. Something he'd read in a psychology book surfaced: *An irrational person's meaning of a situation is different than ours.*

For some reason the woman in the blue jacket thought Jack wanted to harm her. She was stuck in that reality and he needed to yank her out of it. He decided to go completely random.

"My dog needs me!" he shouted.

She stopped squirming and looked up. Her wide brown eyes sparkled with unshed tears of fear. "What?" she said.

"My dog needs me."

"Your dog?"

"If you fall, chances are I'll go with you, because I won't let go of your arm. Then I'll die, or at the very least I'll be injured, and Romeo will be all alone."

"Romeo?" she repeated.

Make a personal connection and/or connect the irrational person back to reality.

"Romeo Albert Garrett Monroe," Jack said.

She frowned, as if trying to figure out what he was talking about.

"I know," he said. "I've been told that's a lot of names for a dog. I'm Jack Monroe. Just two names."

She blinked and was no longer squirming.

"I'm going to pull you up now."

He didn't wait for a response, didn't want to take the chance she'd drift back into hysteria. In one swift motion he yanked her up and her lithe body slid across his and landed on the other side of him.

Flat on his back, an uncomfortable position considering his backpack, he took a deep, relieved breath. Snow started falling again, a little more insistent than today's earlier dusting of flurries.

The woman sat up and scooted away from him. "Who are you?"

He'd just told her his name. Had she forgotten already?

"I'm Jack Monroe," he said. "I'm a volunteer with Mt. Stevens Search and Rescue, K9 unit."

Romeo barked from above, frustrated that he wasn't a part of the action.

She glanced up.

"That's Romeo," he said. "You know my name and his name. What's yours?"

"Zoe. Zoe Pratt."

"Is she okay?" Leslie called down.

"Yes!" Jack responded, although he suspected she wasn't totally okay. He wasn't sure how serious her injuries were.

"Did you find Shannon?" Zoe asked.

"Who is Shannon?"

"My friend."

"Did she fall, too?"

"No, she was…" Zoe hesitated and hugged herself "…taken."

"Taken, you mean…?"

"A big guy attacked us and grabbed her and…" Her voice hitched.

Jack was supposed to do something here, something that would make her feel better. But what?

"They're sending a team to treat your injuries and bring you safely down the mountain," he offered.

She pinned him with intense brown eyes. "No, I'm not leaving without Shannon."

He searched his mind for a logical response. There was none, since staying out here, injured and cold, wasn't sensible. He didn't want to upset her, so he tried something he'd heard before. "I understand."

Although he didn't. This woman might be helpful in the search for her friend, but delaying treatment of her injuries could make her condition worse. At least, her physical condition. He had no idea how to assess her mental condition.

"Because of Romeo?" she said.

"Excuse me?"

"You understand because you love your dog, Romeo?"

"Sure."

He'd initially said he understood her desire not to leave the mountain because that was the appropriate response. Now that she connected her situation to his dog, it actually made some sense.

He didn't like the fact that this irrational and highly emotional woman was making sense to him.

He took off his gloves and pack, and dug for the first aid kit. "You have a cut on your cheek." He tore open an antiseptic wipe and reached out to treat her wound.

"Don't." She jerked away and started shivering. Not from the cold.

Although he wasn't an expert at reading emotion, he knew fear when he saw it. His gut clenched. "I won't hurt you," he said.

She glanced at him with those expressive eyes, hugging her knees to her chest. Her body still trembled.

Although he'd talked her out of her hysterical response to falling, she might still be processing that trauma, or the trauma of seeing her friend kidnapped, or the trauma of... Oh. Something clicked in his brain.

"The man who took your friend," he started, "did he hurt you, too?"

She pinched her eyes shut and nodded.

"Did he push you off the trail?"

"Yes," she said softly.

"Zoe?"

She opened her eyes.

"He's not here now. He can't hurt you."

"He's got Shannon. Please call someone, the police, and tell them what happened."

Jack wouldn't be able to tend to her injuries unless he did as she requested. He clicked on the radio. "Command, this is Jack Monroe."

"Go ahead, Jack."

"The victim says her friend was taken by a stranger, the same man responsible for the victim's fall, over."

"Taken, as in kidnapped?"

"Affirmative."

"I'll notify the sheriff's office. Which way are they headed?"

Jack glanced at Zoe.

"Up toward Prairie's Peak," she said.

He shared the information with base.

"Sheriff's office might radio back for details," Command responded. "This changes things. Be careful."

"Roger, out." Jack hooked the radio to his belt. Unfortunately, making the call didn't seem to ease Zoe's anxiety. "They'll do their best to find her," he said, but stopped before giving her the statistics on such a rescue. Given the criminal element of the situation, combined with weather reports calling for heavy snowfall... They wouldn't be encouraging.

She reached up and fumbled for where her scarf would be.

"We found your red scarf on the trail. Leslie has it above," Jack said. "You can use mine."

"My necklace, where is my necklace?" She unzipped her blue jacket and searched her neck with trembling fingers. "It's a silver dove. It represents the Holy Spirit. I need to hold it, to pray and...

and… Shannon's mom gave it to me when I was thirteen." She shifted around, as if it had fallen off and was lying beside her.

She was growing more agitated. He had to calm her down. "'Have I not commanded you? Be strong and of good courage. Do not be afraid, nor be dismayed, for the Lord your God is with you wherever you go,'" Jack said.

Zoe's fingers froze, and she slowly lowered them. "'… The Lord your God is with you wherever you go,'" she repeated. "You know the Bible?"

"I read everything in my aunt Margaret's house growing up, including the Bible."

She sniffed, a tear trailing down her cheek. Jack needed to do more.

"I will find your necklace," he said, unsure how he was going to make good on that promise. Yet his words seemed to calm her. "I'd like to treat the cut on your head so it doesn't become infected. It might take medics a few hours to get here."

She nodded, hugging her knees tighter to her chest.

He tentatively reached out with one hand and brushed dark hair off her cheek. She closed her eyes as if he was hurting her, although he knew he wasn't. Maybe she didn't like to be touched, especially after everything that had happened today.

Lightly pressing the wipe against her skin, he said, "Did you have a hat?"

"Yes."

She must have lost it when she fell.

Her wound wasn't deep, which was good. It would be a shame if she ended up with a scar on her perfect skin, a reminder of the trauma she'd endured today. Yet she'd survived the fall and apparent kidnapping in fairly decent condition. At least from what he could see.

He took off his own knit hat and placed it on her head to keep her warm. "How about other injuries? Legs, arms, does anything else hurt?"

"My heart."

That concerned him. Was she having breathing issues relating to a collapsed lung? "A pinching feeling or dull ache or…?"

"All of the above." She pinned him with those soulful brown eyes. "I may never see Shannon again."

He exhaled a sigh of relief. "Oh, okay. I thought you'd sustained a serious injury like a punctured lung or cracked ribs."

"What I'm feeling is very serious."

As he studied her expression, an image flashed across his mind.

His parents driving away from Aunt Margaret's house, Jack standing on the porch holding his Lego lunch pail, a peanut butter and honey sandwich with chips tucked inside.

He didn't want to drift back there, didn't want to remember how he'd felt when his parents had abandoned him. He'd spent the last twenty-plus years shoving that persistent ache down where it couldn't hurt him anymore.

Yet here it was.

"I apologize," he said. "What you're feeling *is* serious, but it's not what I was referring to."

She broke eye contact and glanced up at the sky. "Will they keep searching for Shannon at night?"

"The sheriff's office will make that decision based on weather conditions."

She frowned as a few flurries landed on her dark eyelashes. "You mean snow?"

"Snow and wind and available law enforcement personnel to accompany the teams."

"Won't they have a better chance of finding her tonight than if they wait until tomorrow?"

"The decision to proceed with a rescue is determined by both recovery of the subject, and safety of the team. If team members are hurt, that adds to the burden of the rescue. Not to mention this rescue is more complicated because of the kidnapping element."

At the mention of the kidnapping, she hugged her knees even tighter.

Wanting to pull her out of her fearful state, he decided to make an attempt at small talk. "Are you from the area?" he asked.

She shook her head. "No. City girl."

"Which city?"

"Portland."

"And your friend, Shannon?"

"She lives in Mt. Stevens and works at the resort."

"Is she an experienced hiker?"

"Yes. She's the activities director at the resort and part of her job involves taking guests on hiking adventures."

"And she chose to take an inexperienced hiker like yourself out on a winter hike?"

She shot him a look. He must have overstepped.

"You probably want to save details of today's incident for the authorities," he said.

"I, well… It sounded like you were being critical."

There was truth to her assessment. Jack had little tolerance for people who didn't use their good sense, and he was ill equipped to mask his judgment. Another reason why he'd struggled to make and keep friends: his brutal honesty. *It comes with your brilliance, Jackie boy*, his aunt used to say.

Some days, being smart was overrated. As he sat with Zoe Pratt, waiting for help to arrive, he wished he had less smarts and more compassion or understanding or some other characteristic that would ease that tense frown off her face.

Instead, he only had facts.

"Since your friend is an experienced hiker, she will have an advantage over her kidnapper. Unless she's injured," he offered.

Zoe's eyes widened. Perhaps he should have left out the part about her friend being injured.

"Did she have a personal locator beacon?" he asked, trying to recover from his mistake.

"Yes."

"Then her priority will be to activate it." Now he was making stuff up. "Experienced hikers know how to make a fire and stay warm throughout the night."

"Unless she's unable to get away from that jerk." She paused. "Or she's hurt."

Once again, Jack had done more harm than good. He thought it best to keep his thoughts to himself during the remainder of his mission. One thing he knew for sure, the sooner he distanced himself from Zoe Pratt, the better off they'd both be.

Now she knew how her teenage clients felt when they claimed no one was listening to them.

Zoe told rescue workers she wanted to stay in the mountains until her friend was found.

Search and Rescue had denied her request. Their job was to rescue Zoe and bring her to the hospital. If she denied their assistance, she'd be putting the SAR volunteers at risk.

After being checked out by medics at the scene, she'd been assisted down the mountain. *God, please take care of Shannon.*

As she waited in the ER to be officially released, a police officer in his forties joined her in the examining area.

"I'm Sergeant Peterson with the sheriff's office," he introduced. "Are you up to answering some questions?"

"Sure." She shifted into a better position and winced.

"How do you know Shannon Banks?"

"She's my best friend from childhood."

"And you two were up in the mountains because…?"

"A winter hike, to clear our minds."

"Was she upset or concerned about anything in particular?"

"I think she and her boyfriend were having trouble."

"What kind of trouble?"

"She didn't go into detail."

"Where were you headed?"

"Prairie's Peak Overlook."

"Could you identify the kidnapper if you saw him again?"

"Absolutely."

His nodded and checked his phone. "Excuse me, I have to take this."

Zoe leaned back, still trying to wrap her head around it all. This was not how she'd planned to spend her time in Mt. Stevens: Shannon kidnapped by a stranger; Zoe bruised, terrified, and rescued by an enigmatic man named Jack.

He was an odd sort of fellow, asking random questions, then going completely silent as they waited on the plateau for help. Yet when she'd inquire about his work as a search-and-rescue volunteer—how a dog is trained, how many hours of training it takes for a person to be qualified as a handler—to distract herself from her worry, Jack Monroe was Mr. Chatterbox. It seemed like he was more comfortable talking about facts, figures and percentages of lost hikers rescued in the Cascade Mountains than dealing with Zoe's panic about Shannon.

Once she had come down from her emotional spin, she surmised that Jack was highly intelligent and socially challenged, perhaps even on the spectrum. He and his dog with the four names had stayed close to her when SAR helped her down the trail.

Away from Shannon.

Would she ever see her again?

"Hello?" a voice said from the other side of the curtain.

"Yes?"

Jack stepped into the examining area and stood at the foot of her bed.

"Shouldn't you be out looking for Shannon?" she said. Then a horrible thought seized her. "Unless…"

"We've cleared the section of trail up to Prairie's Peak," Jack answered.

"And you haven't found her?"

"No."

"So that's it? You're giving up?" She realized she was being awfully hard on the man who'd saved her life.

"They've temporarily called off the mission due to weather," he said. "If there was any way to continue the search, I would be out there."

"Of course." Zoe sighed. "I wish I knew why this was happening to us."

"Maybe your friend got involved with the wrong people."

She snapped her attention to him. "Excuse me?"

"Your friend got involved—"

"I heard you the first time. Why would you even think that?"

He shrugged.

"Well, it's not true."

"People aren't usually randomly kidnapped without cause."

"How dare you malign Shannon. You haven't even met her."

He just looked at her.

"Well, say something," she said.

"Like what?"

"Like you're sorry for starters."

"You posed the question, so I assumed you wanted—"

"It was a rhetorical question, thank you very much."

A puzzled frown creased his forehead. His suggestion bothered her more than it should, which meant…she sensed potential validity to his comment.

"I'm feeling exceptionally vulnerable and I need people around me that I can trust," she said. She was a jumble of emotions and feared she might completely lose it in front of this stranger. She wanted privacy. She wanted counsel with God.

She needed her friend back.

A man in a dark suit joined them. "Miss Pratt, I'm Detective Perry." He narrowed his eyes at Jack. "What are you doing here?"

"Checking on Zoe."

Zoe felt anxious and confused, both by Jack's accusation and her own visceral response.

"I need to question Miss Pratt," Detective Perry said.

With a slight nod, Jack left her alone with the detective.

"Any news about Shannon?" she asked.

"No, ma'am. I'd like to ask you a few questions about what happened."

"Oh, okay." She wondered how many police officers she'd have to repeat her story to.

"Why were you out hiking today?"

"To clear our minds of stress. Prairie's Peak is a favorite spot of Shannon's and she wanted to share her special place with me, you know, to cheer me up."

The detective waited for more.

"I broke up with my boyfriend a few months ago," she explained.

He nodded, wrote something down in a small notebook. "Can you describe the assailant?"

"A large man, over six feet tall, with an angular face and dark eyes. He was in his thirties with a scar above his left eye."

"You think you could identify him?"

"Yes."

"I'll have you get with a forensic artist. What did the assailant say, exactly? Did he seem to know your friend or call her by name?"

"No," Zoe said. "He didn't say much only…" She reflected back on the moment she decided to catalog every detail about the man. "When he got close, I smelled cigarettes on his breath. I tried to help Shannon and he said, 'This is not your fight.'"

"So, he was specifically targeting Shannon."

"I don't know. I guess it seems that way."

"Then what happened?"

"When I wouldn't let go of Shannon, he said…" the memory resurfaced in a flash "…that I would die with her." She eyed the detective. "You've got to find her."

"We'll do our best. Specialized training is needed to go after a violent criminal in the mountains. We're putting together a few teams, including police officers, that will be on standby for when the weather breaks. We can't let search-and-rescue teams of civilians head up there without police officer escort. It's too dangerous."

She didn't like his answer, but she understood it.

Zoe spent the next fifteen minutes answering the detective's questions about Shannon. It was only then, when Zoe didn't have the details that he seemed to be looking for, that she realized she didn't know as much about the adult Shannon as she should.

Why hadn't Zoe asked questions of her friend? Why hadn't she found out more about what happened between Shannon and Randy, about her job, her social life? She felt helpless and utterly alone.

An hour later Zoe was officially discharged and for some reason she wished Jack would have returned. How silly.

"You are a fortunate woman," the nurse said, then explained how to wrap her bruised ribs and manage the concussion. "Your injuries could've been much worse."

Zoe didn't feel fortunate. Her friend was still out there, cold, vulnerable and probably hurt.

Hopefully still alive.

God, grant me the serenity to accept the things I cannot change… She recited the prayer silently.

Shannon had been violently kidnapped. Zoe couldn't change that fact, but she wasn't powerless. She could pray for her friend's safety. Zoe didn't believe Shan had gotten involved with the wrong people; she might find clues at Shannon's house to assist with the investigation into her kidnapping.

As she waited outside the hospital for a ride to take her back to Shannon's modest home, she considered her next move. Yeah, like what move? Hike up a mountain in the dark with a concussion and bruised ribs to find her friend?

For half a second, she wondered if the concussion was, in fact, affecting her good sense.

A squad car pulled up and a deputy got out. "Are you Zoe Pratt?"

"Yes."

"I'm Deputy Ortman. Sergeant Peterson asked me to give you a ride."

Once inside the cruiser, she decided to press Deputy Ortman for news about her friend. "What's the status of the search?" she asked.

"Three search teams are ready to deploy once the storm passes."

Well, three was better than one. Still…

"How is Shannon going to survive?" she said softly.

"If the kidnapper wants something from her or her family, it's in his best interest to keep her safe."

She kept circling back to the same question: Why Shannon? And who was going to get the ransom call? Her parents were stable financially, but not wealthy.

She wished she had a sounding board, someone to process it all with.

An image of Jack standing at the foot of her hospital bed flooded her thoughts. The unique man who'd saved her life. She had either been brusque with him, or an emotional tornado. She assumed he'd feel safest keeping his distance.

But who could blame her for being an emotional basket case in her situation?

She wondered if Jack was on one of the search teams standing by to look for Shannon.

They had to find her. Zoe wouldn't accept the alternative. Few people other than Shannon knew the real Zoe, understood and loved her, faults and all.

The deputy turned into Shannon's snow-dusted driveway leading to the charming, two-bedroom house. The snow hadn't accumulated nearly as much down here as it had up on the mountain.

Zoe spotted a lone figure standing on the front porch. From this vantage point, it could almost be… Shannon. Hope flared in Zoe's chest.

The deputy parked the cruiser and Zoe thanked him for the ride. As she approached the house, she said, "Shannon?"

The woman pulled the scarf off her face.

"Oh, sorry," Zoe said. "I thought you were Shannon."

The visitor extended her hand. "I'm Kelly Washburn, Shannon's friend. We work together."

"Zoe Pratt."

"No offense, but I was hoping it was Shannon in the back of the squad car," Kelly said. "I heard what happened and had to come over. I don't know why. I had to do something."

"I know the feeling."

"I even brought sloppy burgers, her favorite, from the resort's restaurant."

"That was thoughtful, thanks." Someone with a positive attitude. Zoe liked that. She scanned the porch. "I wonder where she keeps the spare key?"

"It's probably unlocked," Kelly said. "People out here rarely lock their doors. If not, she keeps the spare under the mat."

Zoe twisted the door handle and it opened. Small towns were so different than urban areas. She would never leave her apartment door unlocked. They entered the modest home and Kelly proceeded to turn on some lamps.

Shannon had decorated the open floor plan with simple, comfortable furniture, plenty of throw blankets and insulated drapes. Each of the two bedrooms had its own heater and thermostat, as did the main living area, although Shannon said she relied on the fireplace to warm that space.

Zoe glanced at the fireplace. She and Shannon had stayed up until 1:00 a.m. the first night she'd arrived, reconnecting, talking about their careers, sharing accomplishments and disappointments. They weren't done. They had so much more to discuss. Would Zoe get the chance?

She felt Kelly's hand touch her shoulder. "We need to remain positive."

Zoe nodded, grateful for the kind words. Although she was starting to feel the drain of the day's trauma on her body and mind, she didn't want to be rude. "So, you and Shannon met at work?" she asked.

"Yes, we bonded over our love of hiking, volunteer work and snickerdoodles." Kelly placed the take-out bag on the table.

Zoe sat at the kitchen table but didn't reach for the bag right away.

"Guess this was a bad idea," Kelly said. "I mean, it's not like either of us is hungry at a time like this."

Zoe thought about the colorful snickerdoodles Shannon had packed for their hike. "I should probably eat something since my last meal was breakfast."

"I'll get us something to drink," Kelly said.

"There's juice and soda in the fridge. I'm good with water."

Kelly went to the kitchen and pulled glasses out of the oak cabinet. "How did Shannon seem today?"

"Pretty good. Happy to be going on a hike. Why?"

"I don't know. She'd been distant lately."

"She said she was having boyfriend problems," Zoe offered.

"Couples always have minor bumps," Kelly said.

"Or major ones," Zoe muttered.

"Uh-oh. Recent breakup?"

"Yeah. It's done. I've moved on."

Kelly placed a glass of water in front of Zoe and joined her at the table. "If it was meant to be, it will work out, right?"

"How about you? Do you have a steady boyfriend?"

"Semi-steady."

"I've never heard that term before."

Kelly opened the bag of food and shrugged. "It's still too new to define."

"Ah."

Zoe appreciated the distraction of sitting here chatting about life and guys, almost pretending as if there weren't some larger crisis taking place outside these four walls.

Shannon was gone. Kidnapped by a brutal man.

"What, you don't like the burgers?" Kelly asked.

"Sorry, kind of distracted."

"Hey, give me your phone and I'll put my number in the contacts," Kelly said. "That way you can call me anytime and vice versa."

"Good idea." Zoe handed her the phone. "Tell me more about Shannon's behavior lately."

"She'd been a little withdrawn. I figured that was because of Randy."

Zoe nodded.

Kelly handed Zoe's phone back. "Call me anytime. I mean it."

"Thanks." She opened the bag and pulled out a burger.

A tinkling sound chimed from Kelly's phone. She glanced at it. "The boss." She stood. "I'm sorry, I have to leave."

"No worries. Thanks for coming by and bringing food." Zoe walked Kelly to the door.

Kelly hesitated. "Call or text if you hear anything."

"Absolutely."

Zoe shut the door behind Kelly and sighed. It was nice to have someone to talk to about all this, someone who knew Shannon. It was also good to know that Shannon had friends in town, people who cared about her.

Zoe put the bag of burgers in the fridge. She decided to lie down, rest her sore body and eat later.

"Let go and let God," she whispered. She grabbed her purse off the sofa and opened it. She found the tin of tummy-soothing herbal lozenges and took one, then spotted her canister of pepper spray. If only she'd had it earlier...

She sighed. It did no good to blame herself for

what had happened, even if it felt like it was somehow her fault. She headed toward the guest bedroom, gripping the pepper spray as if she could somehow rewrite history. *"If only" is a diversion from grace*, a minister had once said. How true.

Stepping inside the darkened guest room, she reached for the light switch.

A firm arm wrapped around her neck from behind.

"Where is she?"

THREE

The mission was on indefinite hold. Although three teams were ready to go, the weather had taken a turn for the worse. They wouldn't be going out tonight to search for Shannon Banks.

Instead of heading back to his rented hotel room, Jack sat in his SUV eyeing the small house in the distance. When he'd left the hospital earlier, he'd gotten a call from Leslie that she'd found the silver dove necklace belonging to Zoe Pratt. He'd gone to retrieve it in the hopes it might comfort Zoe, yet now he hesitated to knock on the front door of her friend's house where she was staying. Why?

The woman's fragile emotional state made him uncomfortable. He didn't want to say the wrong thing, didn't want to upset her again. After all, she was still angry with him for speculating about her friend's association with questionable persons.

He eyed the silver dove in his palm. There was no downside in giving her the beloved trinket. Then again, his very presence would remind her that the search had been suspended.

He was overthinking things. Nothing new.

A low growl emanated from the back seat. Romeo sensed something outside.

Jack opened his door. Listened.

He decided it was an owl discussing evening plans.

Romeo barked repeatedly. Maybe he needed a bathroom break. Jack let him out of the truck and the dog bolted past him, sniffing the ground intently. It wouldn't be the worst idea to bring the canine along when Jack encountered Zoe again. Romeo's presence might take the edge off their human interaction.

Romeo bolted up the stairs to the front porch.

Jack started to have second thoughts. What if Zoe thought he was bringing news about her friend? She'd be sorely disappointed and possibly more upset. Yet he wanted to offer her comfort in the form of her necklace. It also wouldn't hurt to recalibrate their relationship with a positive interaction. Assuaging things between them could help Jack become more familiar with her missing friend. If Shannon Banks had been able to escape her captor, Jack understanding her thinking process could potentially expedite the rescue.

He knocked firmly on the front door. Waited. Had Zoe already gone to bed?

He tried again.

Romeo's ears pricked.

Jack studied him. This made no sense. They weren't in the field, weren't tracking scent.

Romeo bolted around the side of the house. Jack followed and found the dog barking furiously at a side window. Jack peered through a crack in the curtains but couldn't see much as the room was pitch-black.

"Come on, before we get arrested for peeping." Jack commanded his dog to accompany him to the front door.

He knocked again.

Romeo anxiously paced back and forth.

Dogs know things humans don't. Words spoken by Jack's mentor and dog trainer, Riley Cooper.

A crash echoed from inside the house.

Jack twisted the door handle. Locked.

He shouldered the door once, twice. Decided not to dislocate his shoulder.

Another crash and a woman's scream pierced through the window.

He scanned the porch for potential spots to hide a key.

Under a planter. No.

Behind the rocking chair. No.

Aunt Margaret hid hers beneath the...

He flipped over the colorful, braided welcome mat and grabbed the key.

"Romeo, wait," he ordered, not wanting the dog to be harmed.

Jack unlocked and flung open the door. A large man charged Jack, slamming the door shut and pinning Jack against the wall. Romeo barked from the front porch.

The man slugged Jack in the gut, then spun him around and applied some kind of choke hold.

Jack shoved the assailant back against the kitchen counter, hoping the pain of making contact would weaken him. Instead the guy clung tight to Jack's neck, putting pressure on his windpipe. Swinging Jack to the right, he smashed Jack's head against the refrigerator.

Jack was not a rag doll to be tossed around at will. He had the strength necessary to free himself. He was not that weak kid anymore.

He jerked his elbow into the guy's stomach once, twice. On the third jab, the attacker's grip loosened enough for Jack to slip out of the hold and stumble away. Sucking in air, he fought to clear the stars from his vision. He had to think, strategize.

The assailant turned, his face red with anger. He had black hair, dark eyes and an angry expression. The guy was about to charge again. Jack scanned his immediate surroundings for a weapon.

"Not happening, dirtbag!" Zoe cried.

The guy turned toward her.

Jack charged him and put a hold of his own on the attacker.

Zoe had other plans. She was aiming what looked like a canister of pepper spray at the guy. "Get down, Jack!"

He pushed off the man and hit the floor. A hissing sound was followed by the guy's howl of pain. From his position on the floor, Jack watched the assailant stumble across the room toward the back door.

"You'd *better* get out of here!" Zoe shouted. She opened the front door and let Romeo inside. The dog took off after the assailant but the screen door slammed shut before the dog could follow him outside. Romeo kept barking and jumping at the back door, wanting to go after him.

"Romeo, stop," Jack said, then glanced at Zoe. "Call 911." He leaned against the wall, finally able to catch his breath.

She knelt beside him. "Are you okay?"

"911," he repeated, not wanting her to waste time worrying about him when police could be in pursuit of the attacker.

She pulled her cell phone out of her pocket and sat beside him on the floor. As she made the call, she scrutinized Jack's forehead and cheeks for signs of injury. The attention made him uncomfortable.

Romeo plopped down, laying his chin on Jack's thigh. With soulful eyes, he looked up, and Jack stroked the dog's head. "It's okay, buddy."

Zoe finished giving a description to the 911 operator and ended the call. Jack glanced at her worried expression. An expression that reminded him of his failures. An expression that made him feel ashamed.

"I'm fine," he said, starting to get up.

Zoe pressed her hand against his shoulder. "Can we wait for paramedics to confirm that?"

"I don't need paramedics."

"You were violently assaulted."

It wasn't the first time, Jack thought.

But it was the second time in one day that Zoe had been brutally attacked.

"Did he…hurt you?" Jack asked, his gut twisting into a knot in anticipation of her answer.

"Scared me mostly."

He nodded, relieved.

"You saved me again," she said.

He shrugged, not knowing if her remark required a response.

"Why did you come back?" she asked.

"To give you this." He pulled the silver dove necklace out of his pocket.

Her face brightened as she took it from him. "Oh, thank you."

"And to apologize," he said.

"For what, being honest?"

"You were angry with me for being honest."

"Actually, I think I was angry with myself."

"I don't understand, but then I don't understand a lot of things when it comes to human interaction."

"I should have done more to help Shannon, for one. Plus, you had a valid point. But if she were in trouble, you'd think she would have told me."

"You live five hours away. Why would she tell you?"

"Distance shouldn't matter. Friends confide in each other."

"Okay."

"What, don't you have any friends?"

Riley came to mind, but no one else. Volunteers he'd met through SAR weren't close friends; they were teammates, work associates.

"You shouldn't have to think about it," Zoe said. The left corner of her mouth turned up slightly.

"You're making fun of me," he said.

"No," she said, touching his shoulder. "I'm teasing, joking around."

When he didn't respond, she continued, "You know, making light of something?"

He knew what she meant, yet in his experience teasing someone made them feel small and foolish. Zoe's comment didn't make him feel that way. This felt…different.

"I didn't mean to offend you," she offered.

He shrugged. "Like I said, I don't always understand people."

"I've been there, too." She reached out to pet Romeo. Jack noticed her hand was trembling.

Although still shaken, she was down on the floor trying to console Jack. He didn't need consoling. He wasn't traumatized by the assault as much as disappointed in himself that he hadn't restrained the guy for police.

"I'm going to get up now," he said.

"Okay, sure." She straightened and extended her hand.

Jack ignored it and stood on his own, wanting to let her know he wasn't seriously injured, and she didn't have to worry about him. From her wistful expression, he wondered if he'd made a mistake.

They sat at the kitchen table and Romeo trotted up to Jack, waiting for direction. Jack pointed at Zoe. "Go help."

Romeo went to Zoe's side and waited expectantly.

"Pet him," Jack encouraged. It always made Jack feel better when his fingers touched Romeo's soft, Bernese–border collie fur.

A few minutes later the tension in Zoe's features softened. Good, it was working.

"Did you recognize the man who broke in?" Jack asked.

"No."

"Did he steal anything?"

"I don't think he was a burglar."

"Why do you say that?"

"Because…" she hesitated "…he said, 'Where is she?'"

"She? As in… Shannon?"

"I guess? This whole thing is so—"

"Puzzling," he said.

"And scary. I mean, one guy kidnaps Shannon

and another is trying to find her?" As she kept stroking Romeo's fur, Zoe's expression grew contemplative.

"Would you like me to make you some tea?" he offered.

His question elicited a slight smile. "Tea?"

"Tea calms the soul." He repeated the phrase he'd learned from Aunt Margaret. Whenever he'd get tied up into knots about kids taunting him, or he felt like an idiot because he didn't know how to interact properly, Aunt Margaret would brew two cups of tea and sit with him at the kitchen table.

"You're an interesting guy," Zoe said.

"So, yes? You'd like tea?"

"Yes, that would be nice."

Good. It gave him something to do, a way to make her feel better. A challenge, since his skill set did not include nurturing.

"I'm sorry about before," Zoe said.

"Before?" He flipped the gas burner on beneath the stainless teakettle.

"Being rude when you said Shannon could have gotten involved with the wrong people."

"I wasn't trying to be malicious."

"I know."

"I'll try to be less insolent next time."

"Interesting choice of words."

A word that his grandmother once claimed defined Jack.

"Why 'insolent'?" Zoe asked.

He pulled two mugs out of the cabinet and formulated an answer, not sure how much he wanted to share.

"Sorry, I didn't mean to pry," she said.

"You apologized for being rude earlier, yet I come off as rude more often than not," Jack said. "It's the way I am. Rude, insolent, impertinent."

"Whoa, which adult used those words against you?"

He turned to her. How could she possibly know?

Sirens echoed in the distance. "Police will be here soon," he said. Excellent timing. He didn't like talking about himself, his childhood.

"You should consider relocating," he said.

"I feel close to Shannon in her home. Besides I want to be here when they bring her back."

Zoe would risk her own safety to be here for her friend *if* authorities found her? It didn't seem like a wise choice to Jack.

"Is there anyone who can stay with you?" he said.

"No, I don't know anyone in town other than Shannon, her friend Kelly and…" she hesitated "…you."

Unfortunate. More people in the house would discourage the attacker from returning. But not just anyone. That gave Jack an idea.

"What is it?" she said.

"Excuse me?"

"You got…" she motioned to her face "…a look, like the gears were spinning in your head."

Wait, she recognized a change in Jack's features when an idea was forming? How could she read him better than most of his closest associates?

"What do you do for a living?" he asked.

"I'm a counselor for adolescents and teens, why?"

That explained why she was able to read him so easily. Counselors were trained to identify feelings buried beneath the surface. He'd have to be more careful with Zoe. He didn't want a repeat of his ex-fiancée, who used her intimate knowledge of Jack against him in the worst way.

"I expect you're good at your job," he said.

"Some days better than others. How about you? What do you do when you're not rescuing damsels in distress from a mountain?"

"IT security. I own my own business."

"I'm guessing that's lucrative."

"Privacy is priceless." He wondered if she caught on to the double meaning.

"That sounds like an ad campaign."

He glanced at her.

"Teasing again, sorry," she said.

"Don't apologize for my shortcomings."

"I don't see it as a shortcoming. Making light of things is simply not something you do. That's okay. So, IT security, rewarding work, is it?"

He suspected she was making conversation to

distance herself from tonight's attack. "Rewarding enough, for now."

"And what happens after now? I mean, you seem like the type of guy who would have a plan."

Of course, it wouldn't take long for a woman in her profession to assess his personality and figure out his *type*.

"My plan is to sell my business and travel the world."

"Sounds lovely," she said.

Her tone belied her words. He wondered why she disapproved.

"You won't miss people when you move away?" she asked. When he didn't answer right away, she said, "You have to have some friends, Jack. Or family?"

"Between the business and SAR, I don't have time for a social life."

Now she was the one to look confused.

Someone knocked on the front door. Romeo charged across the room, and Jack ordered him back to his side.

"It's Detective Perry," a voice called.

Good timing. Jack was growing more uncomfortable by the minute. Sharing intimate details about his life, his future plans, was not something that came easily to him.

Zoe stood and went to let the detective in, giving Jack the breathing space he needed to process their conversation. Regardless of feeling exposed to her in a way he hadn't felt in years, Jack had an intense need to protect her, a woman who touched things in his psyche he'd thought lost or damaged or…nonexistent.

Detective Perry entered with another officer Jack recognized as Sergeant Peterson. Jack was relieved to see the sergeant, considering Perry's obvious dislike of Jack.

"Jack," Sergeant Peterson greeted.

"You again," Detective Perry said to Jack.

"I was returning something to Zoe."

"Something that could be used as evidence in this case?" Perry pressed.

"He brought me my dove necklace." Zoe held it out between her forefinger and thumb. "It represents the Holy Spirit and Jack knew how important it was to me."

"Your timing was convenient." Detective Perry looked at Jack.

"Yes, wasn't it?" Zoe said. "I don't know what would have happened if Jack wasn't here. And Romeo." She reached out and stroked the dog's head. She motioned the two officers to the kitchen table, and they sat down. Jack remained standing. "Jack and Romeo saved me, again." She shot Jack an appreciative smile.

He looked away. This was dangerous, something beyond his understanding. Jack didn't like things he couldn't make sense of or control.

Detective Perry took their statements, including a description of the intruder.

"Midforties, about my height wearing a leather jacket," Jack said.

"He spoke with a raspy voice and had a birthmark on his neck below his jawline." Zoe pointed to her own neck.

"Good thing you had pepper spray," Perry said.

"Too bad I didn't have it with me earlier on the hike."

As they discussed the attack, Jack texted the SAR command chief and asked him to contact certain team members to put Jack's plan into motion. The people he had in mind were perfect for his goal of protecting Zoe.

"So, he was looking for Shannon." Detective Perry's comment was a statement, not a question.

"It's possible, yes," Zoe answered. "Which means she escaped her kidnapper. That's a good thing, right?"

"It could be," Perry said.

"But?"

"There are too many unanswered questions."

"At the very least, the kidnapping and tonight's break-in are related, right?"

"We'd be speculating," Perry said.

"Then speculate," Zoe pushed.

Jack had considered her fragile a few minutes ago, but not right now. Right now she was challenging authorities.

Jack's phone vibrated with a text message. Good, his plan was coming together.

"It would expedite the investigation if we had more detailed information about Miss Banks," Sergeant Peterson said.

Detective Perry shot him a look, then redirected his attention to Zoe.

She continued to pet Romeo, who seemed to be offering comfort. *Good dog.*

"How about problems at work or more specifics about her boyfriend?" Perry said.

"She hadn't heard from him since he went to visit family in Colorado. She didn't talk much about work."

The officers shared another look.

"What?" Zoe said.

"We suspect she was involved in criminal activity, which is the motivation behind her kidnapping," Detective Perry said.

"No, that can't be right," Zoe said, glancing at Jack.

He looked away, uncomfortable at seeing the pained expression on her face.

"What…what kind of criminal activity?" she asked.

"Drugs," Jack guessed.

"Why would you say that?" Perry countered.

"It's logical."

"Is it? I don't think so. I think you know something and you're holding back."

"Detective," Sergeant Peterson intervened. "Jack's been with Search and Rescue for four years. He's solid."

"Everyone's solid until they're not. How's it logical, Einstein?" Perry said.

"Stop!" Zoe put out her hand like she was breaking up a fight between middle school kids. "Why do you think Shannon was involved in drugs?"

"We can't discuss an open investigation," Perry said.

"Fine, then we're done." Zoe stood and planted her hands on her hips.

The men hesitated before standing. "Sergeant Peterson is going to move you to a different location," Perry said.

"No, thank you."

"Ma'am, not only is it not safe for you here, but we need to send a forensic team to dust for prints."

"Pointless," Jack said. "He wore gloves."

Detective Perry glared at him.

"You may leave now," Zoe said, polite yet firm. "I'm capable of taking care of myself."

"Considering what happened tonight, I would have to disagree," Perry said.

"Well, Detective, the assailant is not here, and wherever he is, he's in a world of hurt from my pepper spray. I am unharmed and have more spray in my possession."

"Ma'am, I must insist—"

"Thank you for coming tonight." She crossed the room and opened the door.

The detective hesitated as he passed her. "I can't protect you if you make unwise choices."

"I understand. Good night."

Detective Perry left.

Sergeant Peterson paused by the door and handed her a business card. "My cell number. Call anytime. I can see about having an off-duty deputy watch the house, but I can't make any promises."

"I've got tonight covered," Jack said.

The sergeant and Zoe both looked at him.

"A few SAR members will spend the night until we're called out again tomorrow morning."

"Wait, when did this happen?" Zoe asked.

"You shouldn't put civilians at risk," Sergeant Peterson said.

"Sally Frick and George Connelly are part of the group. They've been informed of the situation. Should be here shortly."

"Ah," Peterson said.

"Ah?" Zoe questioned.

"Frick and Connelly are former military," Peterson explained. "No one's getting in the house if they're here."

"We'll take turns keeping watch," Jack said. "Zoe will be safe."

Zoe will be safe.
Jack's words gave Zoe enough comfort to allow

her to get some sleep. That was, until a nightmare abruptly woke her the next morning.

She struggled to calm her breathing. Glanced around the room. The six-foot-tall armoire had been moved to block the window, probably to prevent the intruder from gaining access to the room.

Low murmurs drifted through the wood door from the living room. She washed up and dressed in jeans and a sweatshirt. She opened the bedroom door to a four strangers with backpacks and bed-rolls. She'd been so exhausted last night that she hadn't heard the team members show up and lay out their sleeping bags on the floor.

"Good morning," she said, searching the room for Jack, but didn't see him.

A woman in her fifties greeted her. "Hi, Zoe, I'm Sally Frick." They shook hands. "Sorry if we woke you."

"You didn't. So, you're the heroes who stayed over to protect me last night?"

"Hero, I like that," said a man in his thirties.

An older man gave him a playful shove. "Who says she was talking about you? Come on, let's move."

"Weather conditions have changed," Sally said to Zoe. "We're meeting law enforcement personnel and heading back up Mt. Stevens to search for your friend."

"Where's Jack?"

"He got an early start with the first team. Sergeant Peterson posted a deputy outside to keep watch of the house, although I think Peterson would prefer you to find another place to stay temporarily given what happened last night. We may not be back for a few days. Weather is looking good."

"Oh, okay. Be careful."

"Thanks, we will," Sally said.

The group of two men, two women and three dogs headed out. Zoe watched them through the window, wishing she could have seen Jack this morning to thank him.

For coming back last night and saving her.

For going out this morning to find Shannon.

For being a grounding presence in her life.

Whoa, back up. The trauma of the last eighteen hours and possibly the concussion must be messing with her cognitive ability. It wasn't like her to rely on a man for stability, especially a man with such opposite views on life.

Jack Monroe was an IT genius who planned to sell his business and travel the world. Where was the stability in that? She had endured too much instability growing up and had made herself a promise never to feel unsettled again. Wasn't that why she and Tim had ultimately broken up? Because his obsession with climbing the corporate ladder and constant, last-minute canceling of their plans left her feeling untethered? She wanted to be able to count on something, someone. Tim wasn't the guy.

And neither was a man like Jack Monroe.

This was definitely her concussion talking. She barely knew the man and had no business thinking of him in those terms.

She turned toward the kitchen a little too quickly, her body aching from the fall yesterday. Well, that and perhaps being yanked around by the creep in the leather jacket last night.

Frustration burned in her gut, as if she'd ingested a handful of chili peppers. While teams were out searching for Shannon, Zoe was stuck in the house doing absolutely nothing.

A familiar feeling of helplessness spread through her chest.

"Oh no, I'm stepping off that one," she said, referring to an expression called the *victim triangle* that her counseling mentor had taught her years ago.

Deciding to be proactive, not reactive, Zoe fixed herself peanut butter on toast for sustenance. As she ate, a plan formed in her mind. She'd search the house for clues, insights into Shannon's state of mind, and maybe even prove that police were way off base suspecting Shan of being involved with drugs. The nerve.

Opening a small, cherrywood nightstand beside Shan's bed, Zoe spotted a pale blue journal.

She turned to the first page, her gaze settling on her friend's fluid handwriting.

She quickly snapped it shut. This felt wrong, like she was violating her friend's trust.

But if it was the only way to gain insight into Shan's life…

"I'm sorry, Shannon." Zoe opened it again and began reading, first the usual stuff—frustration at work, pressure from her parents to move back home—then stories from Shannon's work as a volunteer counselor at a local youth center.

Zoe flipped another page and landed on an entry titled "Randy and Kelly."

I can't believe what's happening. I trusted them with my heart and they betrayed me. Isn't there anyone who loves me and will protect my heart?

"Me, I'll protect your heart," Zoe whispered. She flipped the page.

And saw her own name.

Zoe is coming to visit. I don't know if I have enough energy for her, if I have the strength to comfort her when my own heart is breaking.

Was that how she felt about Zoe? That she was an energy-sucking friend who needed comforting, a friend who sapped Shannon's emotional strength?

"I can't think about that now." Zoe found renewed strength in her determination for answers, especially about Randy and Kelly.

She decided to call Kelly, be pleasant and set up a meeting where Zoe could confront her face-to-face about what she'd read.

"Hello?" Kelly answered.

"Hi, it's Zoe. I need to talk to you."

"I'm actually at the SAR command center prepping food for the team. Why don't you come by and help?"

"Okay."

Kelly gave her the location. "See you soon."

"Thanks."

Zoe left the house and spotted a police officer parked out front. She thanked him for being there, and told him where she was going.

As she drove off, she tamped down her anger so she'd be rational when she questioned Kelly. She considered the possibilities in her mind and landed on the most obvious: Kelly and Randy had a relationship behind Shannon's back.

How could they betray her like that?

She punched the address Kelly had given for the command center into her phone and pulled her compact car onto the main road. She planned what she'd say, intent on being calm, not accusatory. She'd never get answers that way.

* * *

Thirty minutes later Zoe pulled up to the command center and approached the food tent. Kelly spotted her and smiled. "Hi, Zoe."

Zoe couldn't bring herself to smile back. As she was about to question Kelly about the journal entry, a middle-aged man with jet-black hair stepped up beside Kelly. Zoe did not want an audience.

"Zoe?" the man said. "As in Shannon's friend?"

"Yes," Zoe said.

"I'm Curt Underwood, Shannon's boss at Mt. Stevens Resort." He extended his hand. "I'm sick about all this. She's one of my best employees. Please, if there's anything I can do while you're in town. How about I comp a room for you at the resort?"

"Thanks, but I'm staying at Shannon's place."

Curt pulled out a business card and handed it to her. "Call anytime, if you need anything."

"Thank you." Zoe turned to Kelly. "Could I talk to you?"

"Sure." Kelly motioned to Curt. "Can you take over packing the sandwiches for a minute?"

"Of course."

Zoe led Kelly away from the group.

"What's wrong?" Kelly said.

Once they were out of earshot, Zoe turned. "I know about you and Randy."

"Me and Randy?"

Someone touched Zoe's arm. She glanced over her shoulder at Jack. "Jack? I thought you were up searching for Shannon."

"I was." He broke eye contact.

Dread filled her chest. "You mean…?"

She glanced behind him at two men carrying a body bag.

FOUR

Buzzing echoed in Zoe's ears. It was so incredibly loud that she wanted to cry out in pain but couldn't find her voice. Her legs buckled and she went down.

"I've got her," a deep voice said.

And then she was floating, drifting. Unable to hear anything clearly but the rumblings of low voices, her name interspersed between unintelligible words.

It was as if she were having an out-of-body experience, like in a dream when you're watching the situation unfold from the corner of the room, but you're also an active participant in the action.

She blinked against a bright white light glaring directly at her. No, she knew it wasn't her time to meet the Lord. The light faded, and she could see more clearly—she'd been carried under a tent, worried faces of strangers hovered above.

Jack's face. His eyes, usually warm blue, were dark and cold. He looked…angry. Why would he be angry?

Then the muted sounds grew crisp and clear, as if someone had cranked up the volume on the radio.

"Please step back," a man on her left said to Jack. "I need to examine her."

"Go ahead and examine her." Jack didn't move. Dark blue eyes pinned her in place.

A woman stepped up beside him. "Give him space, Jack."

Zoe squeezed his hand tighter. Wouldn't let go. "Jack," she said in a small, strained voice.

"Hi," he responded. "You just fainted."

"Zoe, I'd like to examine you."

She glanced to her left. A man in his sixties with a graying beard and warm smile looked down at her.

"I just fainted," she repeated Jack's words.

"That's probably true, but I'd like to be sure it's not more serious."

She started to feel Jack loosen his grip and she clung tighter. "Jack…stay."

The doctor nodded that it was okay. He took her pulse and watched her breathing, then listened to her heartbeat with his stethoscope.

"Look straight ahead for me."

"She's suffering from a concussion," Jack offered.

"Then it's a good thing you caught her." The doctor checked her eyes with a penlight. "We need to protect that head of yours." He clicked off the light. "Have you had anything to eat or drink today?"

"Peanut butter on toast. Nothing to drink."

"Water," he ordered someone out of view. A

minute later she was presented with a bottle of water and the doctor helped her sit up.

"Stay hydrated," he said. "I think you're okay."

"Thanks."

The doctor left her and Jack alone. Jack's dark eyes had warmed slightly.

"The body bag," she started, "was it…?"

"We haven't identified the body yet."

"Surely you could tell from her clothes?"

He glanced down at his hand, still holding hers.

"She had no clothes?"

"She was wearing clothes, but she'd stripped off her outerwear."

"If she was cold, why would she—"

"In the last stages of hypothermia, something called paradoxical undressing can occur. You think you're hot when in fact you're losing the feeling in your limbs."

She nodded, trying to make sense of what he'd said. "The body you found, it was a woman?"

Jack nodded.

Zoe closed her eyes and said a silent prayer.

"It could be someone else," he said. "Not your friend."

She opened her eyes and sighed. "Have there been other missing hikers reported in the last twenty-four hours?"

He didn't answer, which meant no. Yet he was trying to keep Zoe's hope alive. It was a kind thing to do.

"Thanks," she said.

"Why are you thanking me?"

She shrugged. "For catching me when I fainted, for being a friend."

His brow furrowed slightly, and she guessed he was processing her use of the word *friend* in this scenario.

"Why are you here this morning?" he said.

"I found something in Shannon's diary that disturbed me."

"Her diary?"

She nodded. "I know, diaries are private, and I shouldn't have gone snooping, but I needed to figure out what is going on."

"What did you find?"

"She felt betrayed by her boyfriend, Randy, and her friend Kelly. They did something that hurt Shan deeply."

"Something, like…?"

"I don't know. That's why I wanted to meet with Kelly, to question her."

"You still want to do that?"

"You don't think I should?" Zoe snapped.

His eyebrows furrowed again, as if puzzled by her reaction.

"Sorry," she said. "I'm a little raw right now. I can't believe Shannon is gone."

"The body hasn't been identified yet."

"I… I should be the one to do that."

"You may not want to see her like that, bruised from the fall."

She clenched her jaw against another possible fainting episode. She would not be a wimp about this. "I don't have to identify her by her face, only her right wrist."

"How?"

Zoe hiked her jacket sleeve up to expose the tattoo she and Shannon shared of a cross with a heart. "We figured our parents couldn't be too upset with us for getting tattoos symbolizing our love of God and our eternal friendship. We started with matching bracelets, but you can lose a bracelet, we rationalized. I think Shan still wears hers. Anyway, we got the tattoos."

"Are you sure you're up to this?"

"Yes." Well, she was 50 percent sure anyway. "Is the body…?" She glanced past Jack.

"They've already transported it to the medical examiner's office."

"Then let's go."

Zoe Pratt was more puzzling than trying to figure out a sophisticated DDoS attack, Jack thought as he pulled into the medical center parking lot. One minute she fainted at the thought of her best friend being dead, the next she was intent on identifying the body.

How could someone so fragile be concurrently

strong? Or maybe her strength was a pretense to cover her grief.

He parked and got out to open the door for Zoe. Romeo paced in the back seat. "We won't be long," Jack said to the dog, cracking the back windows.

It would only take seconds to examine the victim's wrist and confirm her identity as Zoe's friend.

And Jack would be ready to catch her again.

As Zoe and Jack headed for the building, Romeo let Jack know he wasn't pleased about being left behind. Jack pointed a finger at the truck. "Quiet." Romeo complied.

"Romeo seems a little bossy today," Zoe said.

"That's the border collie part of him."

"And the other part?"

Jack wondered if she made small talk as a distraction from what was about to happen. "Bernese mountain dogs are gentle giants," he said. "All about love and affection."

"Which mellows out the bossy border collie part?"

"Border collies aren't bossy, they're intelligent. If intelligence is not channeled properly it can be…" he hesitated "…troublesome."

"Not just in dogs."

Was she referring to Jack? There was no way she could know him that well, could she?

"Some of my most challenging clients are teenagers who are off-the-charts smart," she said. "I think intelligence, or even creativity for that matter, can turn sour inside of a person if they don't express it."

"Is it interesting work, being a counselor?" he said.

"Some days. Other days it's…sad."

They paused at the front door to the medical building and he looked at her, about to ask if she really wanted to do this.

"I'm sure," she said, without even hearing the question.

With a nod, he opened the door.

A young receptionist with copper-streaked hair greeted them. She called into the back where they examined bodies and did autopsies. "We have someone here to identify the body found by Search and Rescue… Okay, sure." She hung up the phone and addressed Jack. "They need a few minutes. You can wait over there." She pointed to a small waiting area.

"Thank you," Zoe said, pretending to be sure of herself, pretending to be strong.

Thankfully Jack played along with her mindless conversation, actually asking a question or two, which must have been hard for him. She needed to keep her mind off the dread threatening to consume her. If she looked at the woman's wrist and saw the beloved tattoo…she would be devastated.

Struggling to remain strong, she kept talking as Jack led her to a waiting area with green chairs.

"If you wouldn't mind, I'd like to exchange phone numbers," Jack said. "In case we need to communicate."

"Sure." She handed him her phone.

"I also thought we could activate location services. That way you can track me when I'm on a mission if the reception is good."

And Jack would know where Zoe was, in case trouble found her again.

"Oh, great, thanks," she said.

He added his number to her phone and vice versa, then handed her phone back.

"How hard was it to train Romeo?" she asked.

"Not hard. He has a high play drive and more energy than a toddler. Not that I've been around many toddlers, but I've heard things."

"And why Romeo?"

"You mean the name?"

She nodded.

"Chick magnet."

She almost smiled. "Excuse me?"

"When I first got him, I couldn't decide on a name right away. The vet recommended exposing him to as many people as possible as a puppy and it became clear rather quickly that he was a charming sort of guy. My friend referred to him as a chick magnet, so I named him Romeo."

"Cute."

"You don't like it."

"No, it makes sense. He certainly has won my heart. What about all his other names?"

"Albert is for Albert Einstein and Garrett is for Garrett Morgan, a famous inventor who invented the smoke hood."

"Mr. Monroe?" the receptionist called. "You both may go back now. Down that hall and the first door on the right."

Zoe hesitated before getting up.

"Have you changed your mind?" Jack said.

"No." She glanced toward the hallway, her legs still locked in place, unable to support her.

"You won't need to see her face, just her wrist," Jack reminded her.

With a nod, Zoe stood and took a deep, fortifying breath. Putting it off wasn't going to change the outcome and the sooner she knew the truth, the sooner she could either start the grieving process or continue investigating her friend's disappearance.

The walk down the hall was oddly quiet, her senses attuned to her surroundings: the pale, yellow walls, speckled vinyl floor, and plastic trim around the edges.

Please, God, don't let it be Shannon.

"Should someone else be here?"

Jack's question jarred her out of her desperate thoughts. She glanced at him.

"Other friends or family?" he asked. "We can wait for them."

"Why would I want to wait?"

"For…" he hesitated "…emotional support."

"You're going in with me, right?" she said, sounding a little too needy considering she hadn't even known the man twenty-four hours.

"Yes, I'll be with you."

Silence rang in her ears as they approached the large white door. She could do this. She could be strong for her friend.

Jack paused and looked at her.

"God give me strength," she whispered. Then she nodded and Jack pushed open the door.

A tall man in scrubs stood up from a desk and greeted them. "I'm Dr. Gonzales. You're here to identify the body?"

"Yes," Zoe said.

"She needs to see the right wrist," Jack said.

Zoe shot a quick glance at the glass window, covered on the other side by a curtain. Her heart pounded in her chest.

"One moment." Dr. Gonzales went into the other room.

Zoe took a deep breath and prayed for strength.

The curtain opened to reveal a body beneath a sheet on a table. The doctor went to the body and blocked their view, she assumed to adjust the sheet so only the arm would be exposed.

She could use a boost of strength right now.

Without looking at him, she gripped Jack's hand. He didn't resist the connection.

I can do all things through Christ who strengthens me.

The doctor stepped aside, exposing the victim's bare arm.

No tattoo. No cross and heart.

It wasn't Shannon.

Zoe let out a sigh, not realizing she'd been holding her breath.

"Are you going to faint again?" Jack asked.

She glanced at his worried expression. His blue eyes warmed with concern.

"No, I'm okay."

She didn't seem okay, Jack thought as he drove her back to the command center. Gazing out the window at the towering pine trees on either side of the road, she was taciturn at best, and her pensive expression hadn't changed since they'd left the medical examiner's office.

Although Jack preferred the quiet to nonstop chatter of some people, he found himself missing the verboseness of Zoe Pratt who'd asked him questions about his dog and actually smiled when he'd called Romeo a chick magnet.

Wait, this was no time to be smiling. Then again, she knew her friend wasn't dead, so she shouldn't be too upset, right?

"The victim wasn't your friend. Aren't you…?" He wasn't sure what word he was looking for.

"Happy?"

"No, that's not the word."

"Relieved?"

"Yes, relieved," he said, turning onto the access road.

"I'm very relieved and thankful, but I don't want to get my hopes up too much." She eyed the mountain range bordering them. "Shan's still out there somewhere." She snapped her attention to Jack. "Did you—"

"Notify Command that it wasn't Shannon? Yes."

"How did you know what I was going to ask?"

"It seemed like a logical question. They've sent two more teams up the north side of Mt. Stevens. They're focusing on an old bunker off Trail 415 and Portage Fire Lookout. Sometimes hikers will leave behind food or water bottles for the next person. It's possible Shannon escaped and found shelter and sustenance at the lookout last night."

"If she escaped," she whispered.

"It's a good possibility, considering someone's looking for her now."

She nodded, but it didn't seem like his explanation satisfied her.

"They're doing everything they can," he said.

"I know." She glanced at him. "Sorry about the whole hand-holding thing back there. It was automatic, to reach out for support. I mean, I sense you're not a touchy-feely type of guy and I didn't mean to make you uncomfortable."

"You don't have to apologize."

"You must think I'm a fragile ditz or something. I mean, I'm always leaning on you or fainting on you or holding your hand." She shook her head.

"You're upset about your friend. It's understandable."

This time he meant it. He actually understood. Even though he had little appreciation for emotions, he'd experienced his share of hurt and remorse when he was a child and young adult. It was after his twenty-first birthday that he'd decided to focus all his efforts on shutting down the emotional part of himself and locking it away where it wouldn't be used against him ever again.

They pulled into the command center parking lot. Jack let Romeo out for exercise. Jack wasn't sure if he needed to head back up the mountain at this point, since teams had already been assembled and dispersed. Although he might be able to catch up, something held him back.

Zoe.

He didn't like the idea of her being on her own with the threat still out there.

"I'd better talk to Kelly," Zoe said.

As she headed toward the food truck, Jack walked alongside her.

"Aren't you going back up?" she said.

"I'd like to hear your conversation if possible." He didn't want to get into a discussion about his motivations and why he planned to stay close.

They approached the food tent and found Kelly unloading equipment from the back of a flatbed truck. She saw Zoe and her eyes lit up.

"I heard it's not Shannon." Kelly rushed toward Zoe as if to give her a hug, but Zoe stepped back. "What's wrong?" Kelly said.

Zoe motioned her out of earshot of the rest of the volunteers.

"What was going on between you and Randy?" Zoe asked.

"What do you mean?"

"Shannon thinks you betrayed her, you and Randy together. What's that about?"

Kelly sighed and crossed her arms over her chest. "Oh, so you know about the intervention."

"What intervention?"

"Randy was worried about her and came to me for advice. She seemed…depressed. He kept asking her what was wrong, but she blew him off, said she was fine."

"But?"

"Something felt off. Randy asked Pastor Mike for advice. He suggested we have a meeting, me, Randy, Shannon and Pastor Mike. It backfired. Shannon felt ganged up on."

"When did this happen?"

"A few months ago, around the time one of the

kids from Angie's Youth Club was hospitalized for an overdose. I sensed maybe Shannon felt responsible."

"Why?" Zoe pressed.

"I guess because she didn't realize the girl was using and out of control."

"She never told me."

"That came a few months after another teen from the youth club died in the mountains."

"Was she close to these girls?"

"Very. After our intervention, she slowed things down with Randy and could barely fit me in for coffee. She withdrew from both of us and took extra shifts at work."

Jack watched Zoe's reaction to Kelly's story. Zoe seemed to believe her, but Jack couldn't be sure. Perhaps she was being polite.

"I'd like to speak with Randy," Zoe said.

"I can text you his number, but I don't know when he's coming back. He took it pretty hard when she shut him out."

"Hey, Jack," Sally Frick said, approaching them. "They're putting together another team. You with us?"

He hesitated before answering and glanced at Zoe. Although he wanted to stay and make sure she was safe, he read desperation in her eyes, desperation to find her friend.

"Go on," Zoe said. "Thanks for everything today."

With a nod, Jack turned and joined the team. He had the urge to look back, to make eye contact with Zoe, but wasn't sure why. Instead, he remained focused on the group assembling by the trailhead. He had to concentrate on finding Shannon Banks.

And giving Zoe peace.

As Jack walked away, a chill fell across Zoe's shoulders.

Kelly reached out and touched her arm. "Hey, they're doing everything they can to find her."

Zoe nodded. "I know."

Sergeant Peterson pulled up in a police car. He got out and approached Zoe and Kelly. "Ladies."

"Sergeant," Zoe said. She shot another glance in Jack's direction but couldn't see his dark green jacket among the other team members. He must be leading the charge up the mountain, putting his life at risk to find Shannon.

"I need a moment with Miss Pratt," Sergeant Peterson said.

"Sure." Kelly left them alone and Zoe eyed the sergeant. She suspected he had bad news.

"Although the body they recovered wasn't your friend, we found Shannon's name and phone number written on a piece of paper in the woman's pocket," he said.

"I don't understand. Why would a stranger have Shan's information?"

"We'll know more after we identify the body. We also found drugs on the victim."

"Shannon is not involved in anything criminal, Sergeant."

He glanced down, uncomfortable. She was speaking from a place of faith; the sergeant was trained to consider only facts.

"I can't offer you 24/7 police protection, but I'll do what I can."

"I understand."

"Be careful. Don't go anywhere alone. I'd strongly suggest you not remain at Shannon Banks's house. There are plenty of lodging options here in Mt. Stevens."

"Thank you. I'll look into it." She wondered if he was concerned more about her assisting with the investigation than her personal safety. Okay, now she was growing paranoid. Frankly, she only trusted one person and he'd gone up the mountain to find her friend.

"Ma'am?" Sergeant Peterson said, interrupting her thoughts.

She glanced at him.

"You have my number. Call if you need anything."

Wanting to stay busy, Zoe stuck around to help pack meals for more SAR teams. She found the work both distracting and rewarding. It gave her a reprieve from worrying about Shannon and Jack.

Even though law enforcement had gone up with the SAR teams, she was still concerned about the potential danger waiting for them.

Then she received a text from Jack stating they hadn't found anything of significance. A storm front was brewing up above and the teams were heading back down. She was relieved that he was okay, yet disappointed that they were postponing the search. Again.

The conflicting emotions were taking their toll, so she decided to be proactive and made a reservation at a local bed-and-breakfast. The sergeant was right, she'd be safer in a new location.

She reserved a room at the Ashford Inn, but needed to get her things from Shannon's place before checking in. The thought of going back to the house alone sparked anxiety so she called the sergeant and asked if he could have a deputy meet her there as a safety precaution. He assured her he would.

"Good work today," Kelly said as she passed Zoe.

"Thanks."

Kelly caught up to a group of women and turned back to Zoe. "You have dinner plans?"

"No, why?"

"Some friends are meeting at the Cardinal Café and you're welcome to join us."

"Okay, thanks. I have to check into a bed-and-breakfast first."

"Sounds good."

The camaraderie of being with a group of women would be beneficial, plus Zoe could ask more about her friend's state of mind.

Shannon, why didn't you confide in me? The thought that Shannon considered Zoe the needy one in their relationship disturbed her.

She glanced at the trailhead, but the search teams still hadn't returned. She hoped the weather wasn't making things hard for them. She prayed Shannon had somehow escaped her captor and found refuge.

Zoe walked over to the command chief, Lou Treadwell. "Excuse me, how long before the teams return?"

"Estimated arrival time, forty minutes," Lou said.

"Thank you."

If they were only a few minutes away, she might have waited for Jack.

Really, Zoe? Why? So you can lean on him some more?

This wasn't good. And it certainly wasn't like her. She'd been independent her entire life, starting when her younger brother, Ryan, got sick and she had to pretty much take over running the Pratt household.

Although she could use support during this crisis, she certainly didn't need to depend on a stranger like Jack Monroe to cope with her situation.

Her situation. Shannon had been taken more than twenty-four hours ago.

Glancing one last time at the mountain, she got in her car and headed for Shannon's place. Although she was an independent woman, she felt more than a little lost. Understandable, she counseled herself.

A car honked and she glanced in the rearview mirror at a sedan flashing its lights. She slowed down, assuming he wanted to pass. She surely didn't want to get into an accident on top of everything else.

She rolled down her window and waved him past.

Instead he dropped back.

A car passed by in the oncoming lane. She figured that's why the car behind her hadn't passed. She approached a sharp turn and slowed down. Glanced in the rearview mirror.

And couldn't even see the sedan's headlights, it was so close.

The car slammed into her back bumper.

She started to skid, turned the wheel into the spin, and lost control, veering off into a forested area bordering the road. Her car smashed into a tree and came to an abrupt stop. The force caused the airbag to burst open in her face.

Her head ached with the pressure, and her mind

spun with fear. She fumbled in her pocket for her phone. Couldn't get her hands around it.

The door swung open.

"Is she okay?" a voice yelled from the distance.

"Yeah," a raspy voice called back.

"I'll call 911!" the distant voice shouted.

"Already did," the raspy voice answered. "I got this!"

The airbag was pushed aside and the creep who'd broken into the house last night was staring down at her. "Miss me?"

FIVE

Disappointed. That's how Jack felt when he came down the mountain.

He was disappointed that they hadn't been able to find anything, any clue as to Shannon Banks's whereabouts. He was disappointed that the weather had turned on them.

And disappointed that Zoe wasn't at the command center when he returned. He found himself worrying about her when she wasn't around, and worry was a distraction.

Worry is a waste of creative energy.

He'd said that in a lecture to University of Washington students last year, encouraging them to be bold and think out of the box, even if it meant risking failure. Worry only served to derail a person from achieving their goal.

In this case, finding Shannon Banks.

Jack couldn't control the weather and decided to take his own advice, not worry about Shannon, and perhaps check on Zoe. Sally Frick approached as he packed gear in his car.

"See you tomorrow, then?" she said.

"Or maybe sooner." Jack gazed across the mountain. The weather was so calm down here compared to the intensity of the storm up above.

"I heard it's not supposed to break until tomorrow midday."

"Weather reports can be inconsistent with reality," he said.

"True. Do you need us to bunk at the cottage with Zoe again?"

"No, she's moving to another location. Thanks."

"Anytime."

SAR members packed up and headed out to various locations, either their homes or temporary housing. Their mission wasn't over yet, not until they found Shannon Banks.

As he got into his truck, he wondered how long Shannon could survive up there, either in captivity or on her own. If she managed to escape, she'd still have to navigate the elements.

He'd do an analysis back at his motel room. Right now, he needed to make sure Zoe was safely checked into the Ashford Inn. He called her number but it went to voice mail. He wondered if this was inappropriate, if he cared too much for the stranger with the expressive brown eyes.

He wasn't sure, but he hoped if she felt uncomfortable with his attention that she'd say so. He suspected she would. She didn't seem like, how did she refer to herself, *a fragile ditz*?

On the contrary, there was nothing fragile about Zoe Pratt. She knew her own mind and made no apologies for her decisions. Even if they wouldn't be Jack's decisions, like staying at Shannon's house last night. He was able to acquire protection for her, but what if he hadn't?

When he'd received her text about moving to the Ashford Inn, he'd been relieved indeed. He was glad she told Sergeant Peterson so he could assign patrols to regularly cruise by the inn. Maybe she registered under a different name. That would protect her identity and location. Yet he suspected Zoe wasn't one to misrepresent herself.

He knew little about the Ashford Inn, but after reading the reviews, he thought it a good choice for her, at least for tonight. Unfortunately it didn't accept canine guests, so Jack couldn't stay there, as well.

Would she consider it pushy if he wanted to stay on the same property?

You're thinking too much.

One step at a time. Next step: make sure Zoe was safely settled in.

He directed his phone's virtual assistant to call the Ashford Inn.

"Ashford Inn, Ruthie speaking."

"I'm calling to confirm my friend, Zoe Pratt, has checked in."

"I'm sorry, sir, I cannot share that information."

Irritation quickly dissolved into appreciation.

"Of course, thank you." He ended the call. He'd cruise by the property to see if her car was parked out front.

A few minutes later he spotted flashing lights of two patrol cars near a car that had gone off the road. It wasn't raining so he wondered why the driver had lost control. He shot a quick glance toward the scene.

And spotted Zoe's car.

His fingers clenched the steering wheel. He pulled over to investigate. As he approached her car, he could tell the airbag had deployed and the front end of the car was smashed against a tree. Since he didn't see an ambulance, he wondered if they'd already transported Zoe to the hospital.

A deputy blocked Jack from getting too close. "Stay back, sir."

"Zoe Pratt," was all he could say.

Sergeant Peterson turned. "Hey, Jack." He motioned the deputy to allow Jack access.

"What happened?" Jack said. "Is Zoe okay?"

"We don't know."

"What?"

"We found the car like this, abandoned with no one inside."

Jack thought about that for a minute. "She wouldn't have wandered off, unless she went back to the road and caught a ride."

"Maybe."

"Or maybe what?"

"We received a report from a motorist who saw the accident. He said another motorist stopped to assist. The second motorist said the first one had called 911, but when we arrived, Zoe and the other motorist were gone."

"Did you get a description of the Good Samaritan?"

"The second person who stopped only saw him from behind, but they said he was about six feet tall, had dark hair and wore a leather jacket."

"The guy from last night," Jack blurted out.

"We don't know that for sure."

Jack turned and walked away.

"Jack!" Sergeant Peterson called. "Stay out of it!"

Not possible. Jack wasn't going to sit by and do nothing while Zoe was being tormented. He shouldn't have left her.

No, she wasn't his responsibility.

Trauma flooded to the surface.

Zoe was an adult, capable of taking care of herself. She wasn't a lost and injured teenager. Not his fault. Jack had done everything humanly possible to help her, save her.

The trauma he'd managed to keep locked away suddenly burst free. He got into his truck and slammed the door. Pounded closed fists against the steering wheel, his heart racing.

Romeo whined from the back seat.

"We've got to find her, Romeo."

The dog barked as if he'd understood Jack's words.

Jack thought he'd successfully put that tragic incident behind him. He'd cataloged all the evidence from other SAR members, from the elements, from the Lost Person Behavior resource guide. He and his team had done everything according to proper procedure.

They were still unable to save her. Bottom line.

It didn't seem like other team members, including Sally Frick, were unduly affected by their failure. It happened. Part of the job.

People died.

Zoe's bright, expressive eyes filled his mind. He would not lose Zoe.

He ripped out his phone and did a cursory search. Grabbing his laptop, he opened his locator app to track Zoe's phone. It was more powerful than similar apps and would give him an exact location in real time. Wherever her phone was, he'd find it.

He hoped she still had it in her possession.

A ding indicated the location. The bright red spot on his screen was...

Not far from him. In the middle of the surrounding forest.

Zoe raced through the woods like a woman with her hair on fire. That's how she felt: like her head had been lit up with firecrackers. But she shelved the pain and focused on getting away from the creep.

Good thing she remembered the special karate move Shannon's brother had taught her, the one that never failed to neutralize a male attacker when he was coming at her head-on. It was enough to stun him so she could flee, although she hadn't a clue where she was going.

She still couldn't believe the goon who'd broken into the cottage last night thought she'd surrender without a fight.

She glanced over her shoulder. Didn't see or hear anything. Her attacker must have given up. After all, it wouldn't take long for someone to see her car tangled with a tree and call the police. If the guy didn't want to be identified or caught, he'd have to flee the scene.

Zoe crouched low beside a tree to catch her breath. She had no idea which way to go. She'd been swerving so much she couldn't tell north from south or east from west.

She was lost. It was pitch-black. And she was running out of phone battery. Maybe she had time to make one more—

Then she saw it. The blink of a flashlight.

Had the creep found her?

She dialed 911 in the hopes the little bit of battery she had would enable her to make the call. "It's Zoe Pratt," she whispered as soon as the operator answered. "I'm in the woods. He's coming for me."

The phone went black.

She searched the ground for a fallen branch, anything she could use as a weapon.

The sound of boots crunching on twigs pierced the night. The guy was coming closer.

She grabbed a branch off the ground, the rough bark pricking her skin as she clenched it tight. She pushed up, leaning against the tree for cover and waited.

Snap. Crunch. Snap.

He was only a few feet away.

What if she missed?

Heartbeat pounding in her ears, she rested the branch on her shoulder. She grew dizzy, unsure if it was the concussion or the car crash or both.

Snap.

She pushed away from the tree and swung. Missing her mark, she stumbled forward and nearly fell to the ground.

"Miss Pratt, stop!" a voice said.

A young voice. She spun around.

And was looking at Trevor Willis, one of her teenage clients, wearing goggles on his face. Okay, she was losing it. She'd passed out and was dreaming up this scenario.

"Sorry," Trevor said, removing the goggles. "Didn't mean to scare you."

"What's happening?" was all she could say.

Someone sprang out of nowhere and tackled Trevor to the ground.

"No, stop!" she cried. After all, in this dream sequence, someone was hurting her client. "Leave him alone!" she cried. She swung the branch and it connected with the attacker's back.

In one swift motion he jumped up and ripped it out of her hands. She squinted and covered her face with her arms, expecting the branch to be used on her.

"Zoe."

Her name. Yes, her name was Zoe. But who was—

"Zoe, it's Jack."

She slowly peeked through her arms. A lantern clicked on, illuminating his face. She glanced from Jack to Trevor, who lay on the ground, eyes wide, terrified.

"Why did you attack Trevor?" she asked Jack.

"Who's Trevor?"

She knelt beside the young man, who sat up.

"Isn't this the guy—" Jack began.

"No," she interrupted. "Trevor is one of my clients from Portland. Wait, is this really happening?"

"The pain in my back would suggest it is," Jack said.

"Right, sorry." She turned to Trevor. "What are you doing here, buddy?"

"I was worried about you."

"But how did you—"

"Helen and Dirk are responsible."

"Your foster parents?" Zoe said. "They're responsible for Shannon's kidnapping? But—"

"Who's Shannon? No, I came because I heard Dirk say he was going to put an end to the counselor's meddling."

"We should go," Jack said, scanning their surroundings. "We can discuss this when we're safe."

"You think he's still out there?" Zoe said with a tremble in her voice.

"I'd rather not take a chance."

Zoe helped Trevor stand.

"Hang on." And he grabbed something off the ground.

"What are those?" Zoe asked.

"Night vision goggles," Jack and Trevor said at the same time.

Jack motioned the pair to follow him, then texted his location to Sergeant Peterson.

"Be alert," Jack said to Zoe and the teen, not knowing if the threat was still in the area.

Although Jack was focused on his surroundings, he couldn't avoid hearing the conversation taking place behind him.

"You and your foster parents… It's getting worse?" Zoe asked.

"Yeah."

"Trevor?" she pressed.

"No, he hasn't done that again."

Jack wondered what the teenager meant.

"It's difficult when the people who are supposed to love you don't act loving," Zoe said.

Love. Jack found himself picking up his pace, as if to distance himself from the four-letter word.

"How did you find me? How did you get here?" Zoe asked.

"I tracked your phone."

"Trevor, you're not supposed to use your talents for things like that. It's inappropriate."

"I'm sorry."

"How did you get here?"

"I borrowed Gran's car. I needed to warn you so you'd know to be careful, but then I saw the accident and the guy pull you out of the car and then you nailed him and escaped into the woods. That was rad."

"You should have called the police," Zoe said.

"Then Helen and Dirk would have come for me."

"They don't know you're here?" Zoe asked. "Does your grandmother?"

"No, I didn't want to worry her. I was hoping to come out and warn you, then get back home before everyone figured out I was gone."

"Still, there are better ways to warn someone of trouble."

"You could have called," Jack said.

"Who's this guy?" Trevor asked.

"A friend," Zoe said. "He's good."

"I did call her, but it went to voice mail and I didn't want to leave a message, okay?"

"Trevor, you know how we talk about privacy in regards to what you share with me in session?"

"Yeah?"

"The same goes for me. I deserve my privacy, right?"

"Yeah." The kid sounded disheartened that Zoe was upset with him.

"Jack!" Sergeant Peterson called out.

"Over here!" Jack responded.

"Who's that?" Trevor said.

"Sergeant Peterson."

"Aw, man, not the cops."

"There's more going on here than your paranoia about your foster parents wanting to hurt Zoe," Jack said.

"It's not paranoia, dude."

"It's okay, Trevor," Zoe said. "And thank you for caring so much that you'd drive all this way to find me."

An hour later, back at the sheriff's office, Zoe described the accident and her near kidnapping. Since it was the same guy who broke into the house looking for Shannon last night, authorities surmised this was still about the Shannon Banks case, not a conspiracy Trevor had dreamed up about his foster parents being out to get Zoe.

Detective Perry turned his focus on Jack. "You knew where Miss Pratt was and didn't contact the police?"

"It's fine, he found me. It's all good," Zoe said.

"Ma'am, it's not fine. It's our job to protect you."

"Then where were you when her car was run off the road?" Jack let slip.

Trevor snickered. Zoe shook her head that Jack's reaction was inappropriate. Jack seriously needed to keep his thoughts to himself.

So many things seemed inappropriate lately, beginning with the accusations leveled against him. He wasn't exactly sure what the detective's purpose was. Jack had found and rescued Zoe. Wasn't that everyone's goal?

"Jack," Sergeant Peterson said. "This is a police matter."

Jack was being shamed, in front of Zoe, her teenage client and Detective Perry. "I did what I thought was best for Zoe."

"And I'm okay," Zoe said. "Shouldn't we be focused on getting Trevor home?"

"We left a message for his foster parents," Detective Perry said.

"Great," Trevor muttered.

"Kid, this is serious stuff," Perry said. "You insinuated yourself into a police investigation."

"He was trying to protect me," Zoe defended.

"Do you have any idea what your dad meant, what he had planned in regard to Miss Pratt?" Detective Perry asked Trevor.

"No, but I think he'd do anything to keep her out of court."

Detective Perry glanced at Zoe.

"I'm scheduled to go before a judge in two weeks to discuss custody issues," Zoe said. "Trevor's grandmother is filing for custody."

"There must be pretty serious abuse if you're recommending he be removed from his foster parents' house," Detective Perry said.

Zoe didn't respond. Jack figured it was part of the counselor's code of ethics to keep things confidential.

"Dirk beat me and locked me in the shed for two days." Trevor glanced down, as if he felt somehow responsible for his foster father's behavior. As if he deserved it.

"Sorry," Detective Perry said.

"Why don't you call his grandmother and see if she can come get him?" Zoe suggested.

Detective Perry had Trevor write down his grandmother's number. "I'll be right back."

Perry and Sergeant Peterson left the conference room.

"It'll be okay, Trevor," Zoe said. "I truly appreciate your concern."

"But I shouldn't have come," he said softly.

"You were brave," Jack blurted out.

Zoe and Trevor both looked at him.

"Going against your foster parents' wishes, wanting to rescue someone, even though you knew it could get you into trouble," he continued. He didn't know where the words were coming from.

Jack finally sat at the table with them. He fingered the night vision goggles. "Homemade?"

"Yeah."

"Rad," he said, repeating the kid's word.

Trevor's frown eased a bit.

Jack wasn't sure how, but he was successfully engaging with the young man, who was both bright and caring. An intriguing combination.

"Jack?"

He glanced at Zoe.

"How did you find me?"

"Tracked your phone."

"Hey, that's not fair," Trevor said.

"Trevor," she started. "You're my client. Jack is my friend. There's a difference."

She just referred to Jack as her friend. Did she mean it, or was she trying to illustrate a point for the teenager?

The door opened and Sergeant Peterson poked his head into the room. "We've reached Trevor's grandmother and she's on her way to get him."

"How? I've got her car," Trevor said.

"A friend is driving her."

"Any word from his foster parents?" Zoe asked.

"None."

"Let's hope Gran gets here first," Trevor said.

"Jack, can I have a word?"

Jack stood and went out into the hall with Sergeant Peterson.

"Perry is steaming mad and considering bringing charges against you," Peterson said.

"For what?"

"Interfering with an open investigation."

"Because I wanted to help Zoe?"

"Because you didn't keep us in the loop."

"I was in a hurry."

"Look, I told him you meant well, but you have to keep your distance."

"Someone needs to help Zoe if you can't offer 24/7 protection."

"True, but you can't help her if you're in jail." Peterson hesitated. "I've got an idea. Since we don't know what Miss Pratt's role is in all this—"

"Meaning you think she's involved in drug smuggling?"

"Let me finish. I could tell Perry that by keeping an eye on her, you can get us valuable intel—"

"No."

"Jack—"

"I won't spy for you."

"You can't protect her from lockup either."

"He has no cause to arrest me."

"That won't stop him. Look, I'm on your side. This way everyone wins. You stay out of jail and protect Miss Pratt, she'll be safe, and we get information—" Peterson put his hand up to stop Jack's protest "—if you deem it important to share. Okay? Tell me what you discover. You won't have to deal with Perry. Just think about it?"

Jack didn't need to think about it. He had no intention of betraying Zoe's trust. But still, he appreciated the sergeant's efforts.

"I'll think about it," he said, and went back into the conference room.

It was nearly midnight when Trevor's grandmother arrived to pick him up. Zoe was exhausted both physically and emotionally. Jack offered to drive her to Shannon's place to retrieve her things, and then to the Ashford Inn.

A combination of things had zapped her energy: the constant threat lurking in the shadows; concern about Shannon; and worry about Trevor once he got home. She felt like a robot going through the motions to get her from point A to point B.

So much had happened today and she hadn't had enough time or space to process it all.

"He'll be okay," Jack said.

She glanced at him across the front seat.

"Trevor," Jack clarified.

"Why do you say that?"

"He's a strong kid."

She nodded. "Is there any update on the search for Shannon?"

"They'll head out again after the weather breaks, probably tomorrow afternoon."

"They? What about you?"

"Once I'm convinced you're safe, I will rejoin a search team."

"You shouldn't stay back on my account."

"You need protection."

Crossing her arms over her chest, she felt a slow burn creep up her cheeks. "I think I've done pretty well on my own."

"I agree."

"Then why are you—"

"I don't like to leave things unfinished. I like to see them through to the end."

"O-kay." So this was about his process. It had nothing to do with how he felt about Zoe.

You've known him twenty-four hours, Zoe, not long enough for him to develop genuine concern for you.

"Plus I don't want to see you hurt again," he added.

On the other hand, that was an awfully intimate confession from a man like Jack.

"Thanks." She glanced out the window. "It's nice to know someone's looking out for me. I'm usually the one looking out for everyone else."

"Like your clients?"

"Yes."

"You can't fix them. You know that, right?"

"I knew that when I pursued this profession." *But it still doesn't stop me from trying.* Ugh. Old habits died hard, didn't they? She didn't like that Jack could read her so well. "You know about not being able to fix people from personal experience, do you?" she asked.

"Not exactly, but I read a lot. How long will it take you to gather your things?"

"Ten minutes should do it."

"It might be too late to check into the inn," Jack said. "Some bed-and-breakfasts have check-in rules so you don't disturb the other guests."

"Makes sense. Where will I find a room at this time of night?"

"I booked you a room at the hotel where I'm staying." He glanced at her before she could pro-test. "As a backup. Just for tonight."

"You didn't have to do that."

"I know."

Zoe felt she was being rude again, ungrateful that Jack had thought ahead and planned for her, taken care of her. She wasn't used to it. "Thanks."

"You're welcome." He pulled onto Shannon's street and narrowed his eyes as he focused on the house in the distance.

"I'm not usually this ungrateful," Zoe said. "I'm sorry."

"Don't apologize."

"But—"

"Did you leave lights on?"

"I don't remember, although Shannon might have timers because she works late shifts." A light glowed from the main living area.

He parked about a hundred feet away, not in front of the house.

"Stay here," he said. "Lock the doors."

"Wait, you think—"

He slammed the car door on her question.

"So bossy," she muttered.

Romeo whined from the back seat.

"You think so, too, huh?" She reached back and petted his soft fur, keeping her eyes trained to the house in the distance.

She didn't like this, didn't like the adrenaline flooding her body, or the pitch-black surrounding the truck. She could, however, make out Jack's form as he approached the front door.

Then she saw a flash of something else: a person racing from the house.

Wearing a bright orange jacket.

"Shannon?" Zoe flung open the door and got out. "Jack!" she called, but he'd already gone inside. She started toward the house, wanting to tell him what she'd seen. The front door swung open.

"Get back!" Jack shouted.

Registering alarm on his face, she turned and ran, terrified to her core. She sprinted faster than she thought possible across the snow-covered lawn. Romeo barked furiously from inside the truck.

An explosion reverberated behind her and she instinctively hit the ground.

SIX

Ringing echoed in her ears. It took Zoe a few seconds to regain the breath that had been ripped from her lungs.

Take your time. Advice she'd offered her clients many times.

The sound of burning wood crackled behind her.

Had someone blown up Shannon's house? And what about Shannon? Was that her racing away? Did that mean she could be responsible for—

No, Zoe wouldn't go there.

She scrambled to her feet and saw flames consuming the house. She pulled out her phone and called 911. "An explosion," she said, and gave the address.

Then a horrible thought seized her. Where was Jack?

She scanned the surrounding property but didn't see his green jacket against the white snow.

"Jack," she said. Panic took hold despite her calming efforts. She rushed toward the house, trying to find a safe way to see inside and make sure he wasn't there.

And if he was…

"No!" She stopped short of the house as the heat of the flames warmed her cheeks. There was no way to help Jack if he was inside, no way to save him.

Yet he'd saved her many times in the few days they'd known each other.

She paced back and forth in front of the burning house, trying to make sense of it all.

"Get back!" A firm hand gripped her arm.

She looked up into Jack's rich blue eyes.

"What are you doing?" he said. "It's not safe here."

Still holding her arm, he led her away from the blazing flame, the heat making her eyes water.

Or was something else making them water?

They approached his truck and Zoe leaned against the front grille.

Jack examined her. "Are you okay?"

She shrugged, indicating she wasn't sure what she was. His eyes darted from left to right, then up and down, as if his brain was calculating something and trying to come up with the correct answer.

Then he looked straight at her. She felt a warm tear trickle down her cheek. She nodded, as if she knew what he was considering.

He pulled her into a hug.

Yep, that was what she needed. The knot in her gut eased and she sighed, welcoming this nurturing moment. It wouldn't last long; it shouldn't last long because it would obviously make Jack uncomfortable.

Plus, she didn't want him to think her weak.

"Thanks," she said, and pushed away.

"Why were you trying to get into the house? Were you trying to get your things?"

"No, I thought you were inside."

He frowned, probably thinking she didn't stand a chance of helping him even if she'd gained access to the house, so why put herself in that kind of danger? She couldn't analyze her motivations, not now, not with her emotions in a tangled mess. Instead, she changed the subject.

"I think I saw Shannon." She wasn't sure if she should tell Jack or the authorities, but she knew at the very least she wanted him to know.

"Where?"

"Running away from the house."

Jack shot a puzzled look toward the burning home. "Are you sure it was her?"

"No, but the person was wearing her orange jacket and they were the right height."

"Hair color?"

"Wore a ski cap."

They both gazed at the flames consuming the small structure.

"Why destroy the house?" Zoe asked.

"To destroy evidence."

"Shannon is not a criminal."

"We don't know for sure the person fleeing the scene was Shannon."

The sound of sirens grew louder. It was a blessing that Shannon's house sat on half an acre, not too close to another home.

He studied her face intently.

"I'm okay," she said, sensing he thought she needed another hug. She didn't want to keep making him uncomfortable just because she needed compassion.

"Get in the car with Romeo," he said, motioning her to the back of the truck.

"Oh, okay." She didn't argue. She sensed he was trying to protect her, or make her feel better, or a little of both.

He opened the door and she slid in beside Romeo. The dog automatically nudged her shoulder, and Jack shut the door. Although it was comforting to have the dog as her companion, she also liked having Jack close. She wondered what he was going to do now. Manage questions from neighbors? Answer questions from police who were sure to arrive any minute?

The opposite door opened, and Jack got into the back seat with Zoe and Romeo.

"I've notified authorities that we're waiting to give our statements when they arrive," he said.

"Thank you." A few seconds passed. "I guess I'll have to go shopping tomorrow."

Jack illuminated the car with a phone app and looked at her.

"What?" she said.

"I'm trying to determine if you were joking or being serious."

"Yeah, I guess that was a strange thing to say, especially when you consider we both could have been inside when…" She made an exploding sound with her mouth. "Uh, I'm so tired I'm not making sense."

"Studies have proven that people who are overly tired can have difficulty processing thoughts and suffer from an inability to concentrate. Long-term effects increase the risk of heart disease, high blood pressure, depression and a weakened immune system."

"Wow, I'm glad my sleep deprivation is only temporary, due to stress because my best friend was kidnapped, someone assaulted me, tried to kidnap me, and then set fire to Shannon's house."

He narrowed his eyes.

"Yes, I was being sarcastic," she explained. "Sorry, I think it's a coping mechanism."

"You need to sleep."

"That would be nice."

"You need to feel safe in order to sleep."

"True."

"Which is why I will stay with you tonight."

"Look, I appreciate everything—"

"Police have arrived. Wait here."

Before she could open her mouth to protest, Jack was gone again, managing the situation, her situation. She sighed and petted the dog, unable to gather the strength to chase after Jack and argue his decision to play bodyguard.

She didn't need that kind of help, did she? Had someone torched Shannon's house to destroy evidence of wrongdoing? Or were they hoping Zoe was in the house?

The thought spiked her adrenaline. She didn't want to be inside Jack's truck waiting for the next thing to happen. She was a fighter and continued to fight even when the battle seemed hopeless.

Even when specialists had told her family that her little brother probably wouldn't live to see his tenth birthday.

When her parents failed to pursue any and all options, Zoe had taken over. She did the research, investigated new studies into treatments for Ryan's rare disease. Sure, she had eventually surrendered; if God needed Ryan in heaven, then Zoe would have accepted that outcome.

But He hadn't, because Ryan was alive and well, married and raising two adopted children with his wife, Adele. Because Zoe hadn't given up on his situation.

She wouldn't give up on Shannon either, no matter what evidence presented itself.

But in this moment, she'd relax and pet the dog. She'd pray for God to fill her heart with love, not fear, and prepare herself for questioning from the detective.

* * *

"She's exhausted and needs sleep," Jack said to Detective Perry.

"She needs to come to the station and answer questions about what happened here tonight."

"I'll answer your questions."

"Are you covering for her?"

"There's nothing to cover. Her friend was kidnapped, Zoe was nearly kidnapped herself, and now the house has been destroyed. She's a victim, not a perpetrator."

"Sergeant Peterson said you'd get information from her, correct?"

Jack's answer could land him in jail on obstruction charges where he wouldn't be able to protect Zoe.

"Yes, I said I'd share pertinent information with him, should it come to my attention."

"Is there anything pertinent about tonight?" Perry said, with an edge to his voice.

"I went inside the house and smelled gas. It was strong. I fled the house and it burst into flames."

"And where was Miss Pratt?"

"I told her to wait in the car."

"Why?"

"I wanted to make sure the house was safe before she entered."

"Then what?"

"I saw her walking toward the house and shouted for her to get away. I hit the ground when I heard the explosion."

"Did you see anyone or notice anything?"

He'd seen Zoe racing toward the burning building. He couldn't figure out why.

I thought you were inside.

Zoe's words puzzled him.

"You saw something?" Detective Perry interrupted Jack's analysis of Zoe's actions.

"No, but Zoe said she saw a person run from the house, wearing Shannon's jacket."

"I need to speak with Miss Pratt. Now."

Might as well get this over with. Jack led the detective to his car and opened the door.

Zoe's eyes were closed. She looked peaceful, content. Romeo lay across her lap.

"Miss Pratt?" Detective Perry said.

Jack wished he'd wait until tomorrow. "Zoe?" Jack tried.

She awoke with a start and gasped. Romeo sat up, watching her. "Shannon?" she said, glancing at Detective Perry. "Did you find her?"

"No, ma'am. I'd like to ask you about what happened tonight."

"Tonight," she repeated, obviously still trying to process whatever dream she'd been wrenched out of. "We came to get my things. Jack told me to wait in the car. Then I saw…" she hesitated "…a person who I thought might be Shannon running from the house. I went to tell Jack." She caught Jack's gaze and he had to look away. "He told me to run. I heard an explosion. The house was, is, on fire."

She looked beyond the detective at firefighters working to put out the blaze.

"Why did you think it was Shannon running from the house?" Detective Perry said.

"The person was wearing Shannon's orange pumpkin coat."

"Pumpkin coat?"

"I teased Shannon that the jacket made her look like a pumpkin. It's pretty bright."

"Any other descriptive details?"

"Black knit cap. That's it, sorry."

"I'll put out an alert. Where will you be staying?"

She glanced at Jack. Detective Perry glared at him.

"We're staying at the Blue Cedar Motor Lodge," Jack said.

"We?" Perry said.

"Yes," Jack said. "Are you finished asking us questions?"

"For now."

Jack nodded at Zoe and shut her door. As he went around to his side of the car, Detective Perry shadowed him.

"I don't trust you," Perry said.

"That is your prerogative."

"Listen." Perry stepped in front of him. "I could have held you for obstruction, but I didn't because

Peterson said you'd help us out. All you need to do is earn her trust and relay important information to me."

"And if she doesn't have any important information?"

"We'll decide what's important."

"Understood." What Jack understood was that Perry was another version of the bullies he'd dealt with his entire life. Only Jack wasn't about to cave to this one. He was putting Zoe's best interest before that of a detective who, for some reason, seemed to think she was involved in the kidnapping case.

Detective Perry still blocked him, staring him down, trying to intimidate him.

Jack didn't respond, didn't clench his jaw or narrow his eyes. He knew any reaction would fuel the man's aggressive nature.

"Houses don't randomly explode. We have to assume this was intentional."

"I concur."

"Don't try to be a hero," Perry said. "It didn't work before, and it won't work this time."

Although the mention of Jack's failure at being unable to save the young woman last year would have normally twisted his gut into knots, he considered the source of the barb. Detective Perry was trying to manipulate and control him.

Jack stepped around the detective and got into his SUV.

* * *

The next morning Jack paced outside the bedroom door in the suite he'd rented for Zoe, having canceled his original reservation. Romeo had spent the night in the bedroom with Zoe, while Jack stretched out on the sofa in the main living area. He got maybe five hours of sleep, which would be enough to sustain him through the day.

He still hadn't received a call from Search and Rescue. A part of him was relieved. He didn't want to leave Zoe until he knew she was safe.

He needed to let Romeo out to do his business, but didn't want to awaken Zoe. He tapped softly on the bedroom door. Romeo offered a yelp in response. Jack cracked open the door and Romeo skirted out.

Jack cast a quick glance in the room. Zoe was still asleep, buried beneath layers of bedding.

Jack took Romeo outside, across the parking lot to a small patch of grass where he could keep an eye on the door to his suite. His and Zoe's suite. She had made it clear last night of her intention to pay half the rental fee. Jack was starting to understand that Zoe was a woman who relied on herself first and foremost, that she didn't like asking for or accepting help from others.

Jack sensed most people liked having support from others. At least he'd seen that with his SAR friends, how they gave each other rides, shared snacks and supported one another when field-testing their dogs.

Being a loner himself, Jack could relate to Zoe's need for distance, yet it seemed out of character for a woman like her to shun support and friendship. She seemed to enjoy Shannon's friendship, so maybe she needed to deeply trust a person before she would allow herself to rely on them.

Yes, that had to be it. She didn't know Jack well enough to trust him fully, although she seemed to accept his quirks more than most new acquaintances in his life.

Because that was what she was, an acquaintance. Not a friend. Jack didn't have true friends, nor girlfriends. No, his ex-fiancée had been enough for him. The Mari experience had taught him never to open up again, that even if he wanted to be like other men, he couldn't change who he was—a man with missing pieces.

You'll never able to satisfy a healthy woman emotionally, she'd said, then enlightened him about love, explaining that if he cared about her, he wouldn't imprison her to an emotionless marriage.

To Mari, being with Jack felt like being in prison.

He shook his head to snap out of it. Apparently lack of sleep caused the dark memories to surface, reigniting the pain as if it had happened yesterday.

Then again, maybe it was the lack of sleep coupled with something else triggering his analysis. The way he felt about Zoe Pratt. Concerned. Protective. And something he couldn't quite articulate.

No reason to analyze things beyond his understanding. They had a full day ahead of them, and neither of them knew what would come next.

He grabbed dog food from the truck and went back into the suite.

"Hey," Zoe said from the kitchenette.

"Did we wake you?" He shut and double locked the door.

"No, I had a nightmare."

"I'm sorry."

She looked at him and smiled slightly.

"What's wrong?" he said, dumping kibble in a bowl and placing it on the floor.

"I just… Never mind."

"It makes me uncomfortable when I can't interpret facial expressions. I thought you smiled."

"I guess I did." She poured herself a cup of coffee. "Thanks for making coffee."

"So why did you smile?"

She sat down at the kitchen table. "You held space for me. That's unusual for someone like you."

"Someone like me," he repeated, pouring himself coffee. "You mean…?" All the names he'd been called since childhood started spinning in his head: *Brainiac, freak, dork.*

"Brilliant, gifted, astute," she said.

He stepped around the table to read her expression, wanting to assess if she was being ironic or not.

"This is my authentic, honest face," she clarified. Again, with a smile. "Why do you look so bewildered?"

"Brilliant, gifted and astute aren't usually the first words that come to mind when a person is describing me."

"Ah, you mean people usually focus on the socially awkward aspects of your personality."

He sat across the table from her. "That is correct."

She waved her hand in dismissal. "People get offended if you don't respond the way they think you should. I'll admit I was at first, until I got to know you better. Whatever happened to giving someone another chance or turning the other cheek?"

"The book of Matthew," Jack said.

"You're a man of faith?"

"Not exactly, but I've read the Bible front to back."

"Oh," she said.

He thought he heard disappointment in her voice.

"Thanks again for letting me stay here, but I'll move to the inn later today." She paused. "After I get some clothes and a toothbrush and comb and everything else that burned up in the fire. Which still has me mystified."

"I spoke with Sergeant Peterson. Initial reports indicate the fire was intentional."

She shuddered.

"I'm sorry, I shouldn't have told you that," he said.

"No." She reached out and touched his arm. "Tell me the truth, always. Even if you think it will upset me. Do they have any idea who set off the explosion?"

He hesitated.

"Go on," she prompted.

"If you saw Shannon fleeing the scene—"

"I didn't say it was Shannon."

"But a woman fitting her description was seen leaving the scene. They suspect she set the fire to destroy evidence."

She leaned back, breaking contact with him. "I won't accept that. Ever." She stood and went into the bedroom.

Jack continued to process their conversation about understanding, or rather others' lack of understanding of how his mind worked. He also puzzled over her directive to be completely honest with her. In his experience people didn't always appreciate honesty.

Zoe rejoined him in the kitchen and placed a light blue journal on the table. "They didn't get

Shannon's journal. I'm going to use it to figure out what's going on and why she was kidnapped."

"No," Jack said.

"Excuse me?"

"You shouldn't involve yourself in the investigation. Let the police do their jobs and find Shannon."

"The police think she's involved with drugs."

"They will uncover the truth."

"Wait, you agree with them?"

"I didn't say that."

"It sounded like it."

"I have no evidence either way, so I have no opinion."

"Well, she's my friend and she's in trouble, so I *do* have an opinion. She's innocent of any wrongdoing and shouldn't be blamed for her own kidnapping." Zoe's voice raised in pitch.

He wasn't sure what he'd done to cause her to be upset.

"They should be focused on saving Shannon, not tying her to a drug operation," she said.

"That's not what they're trying to do."

"It sure sounds like it to me."

"Because you're being overly emotional."

She stood so quickly her chair tipped over. Romeo barked as he dodged out of the way of the falling chair.

"Oh no, Romeo, I didn't hurt you, did I?" she said, kneeling beside him.

As she stroked the dog's fur, Jack realized he'd crossed the line again. He'd been too blunt even for Zoe Pratt, who claimed to understand and wanted complete honesty.

"What I meant was—" Jack started.

"It's okay. You're right. I'm being overly emotional." She glanced up at Jack. "I still need to help Shan, at least by finding answers to prove she isn't involved. Can't you understand that?"

He wasn't sure he did, but he wanted to try. "Sure, okay."

"I won't do anything dangerous. I'll make some calls, talk to some of her friends and coworkers. Get to know my best friend," she said, a sadness in her voice.

"I'd like to help." Jack found Zoe intriguing and amiable. He didn't want anything bad to happen to her, and not because he feared failing again. This felt different. She was pleasant and respectful of him.

Whether she wanted to admit it or not, she needed his support.

"Don't you need to go up with SAR to search for Shannon?" she said.

"They haven't sent out an alert yet. As long as I'm not on the mountain, I'll be with you."

Zoe and Jack made a trip to a local retail store that sold everything from fresh produce to clothes. Jack had even managed to find a new canister of pepper spray, in case she'd used up her original. She picked up essentials, plus a couple of pairs of jeans and some tops.

Then Zoe spent the rest of the morning going through Shannon's journal and coming up with a list of people to talk to. She didn't let Jack read the journal per se, because even she felt guilty about peeking into her friend's most private thoughts. But making the list was a good start, and made her feel like she wasn't so helpless.

A part of her wondered if Jack was humoring her, if he thought the journal could reveal answers. Sometimes even she couldn't figure out what was going on in that mind of his. Which was okay. Zoe appreciated that she wasn't doing this alone, and she sensed he didn't have a malicious bone in his body. Instinct told her his motivations were honorable.

Jack focused on work, creating a proposal for a prospective client, and developing code for another. The most Zoe understood about computers was how to turn one on and use her word programs to create assessments, plus how to check email, although she mostly did that on her phone. She received an email from Trevor stating he was staying with his grandmother for a while. Zoe sighed with relief and shared the news with Jack.

A while later, a forensic artist stopped by to work with Zoe on her descriptions of the kidnapper and home intruder. After the artist left, Jack made them both tea and continued to work on his laptop.

"I'm sorry, I forgot you have a life outside of all this," Zoe said.

"Why are you sorry?" He turned to her and leaned against the counter.

She was momentarily distracted by his good looks. Boy, did she need a full night's sleep. "I'm sorry because I'm taking you away from your work."

"It will still be there later. Tomorrow. Next week."

"Do you like your work?"

"I like the challenge, yes. Plus, I like helping clients keep important information secure."

"You're quite a giving kind of guy."

He shot her that cute frown that indicated he didn't know how she'd come to that conclusion.

"Well, you help protect your clients, you help find missing hikers. How did you get involved in Search and Rescue?"

"Romeo needed a job." He glanced at the dog. "Turns out I like the physical challenge, as well."

"When you sell your company and travel, won't you miss Search and Rescue?"

He shrugged. "I'm ready to start today's investigation. Where to first?"

She found it interesting that he wouldn't answer her question. "I thought we'd start with the community center. Shannon volunteered there with the teen program."

"Very good."

Jack left Romeo at the motel and swung by a burger place for lunch. The community center didn't open until 1:00 p.m. so they had time. Sharing a quiet lunch, Zoe realized she was too tired to make mindless conversation, and Jack probably appreciated the stillness.

They occasionally made eye contact, but it wasn't awkward. The silence seemed to satisfy them both. It gave her time to think about what she'd ask employees at the community center. It also gave her time to reflect.

As long as I'm not on the mountain, I'll be with you.

She considered Jack's words from last night. His promise both calmed and worried her. She liked the idea of having personal protection, but she also suspected he was one of the best search-and-rescue volunteers available. He should be out there looking for Shannon, not babysitting Zoe.

"Still no text from SAR," he said. "The weather must be dangerous up there."

The timing of his comment was incredible.

"Well, let's see how much we can get done together before you're called out again," she said. "I should probably contact someone about having my car fixed."

"I believe the sheriff's office took it to process for fingerprints."

She nodded. "Don't suppose you know where I can rent a car?"

"Move that off the list."

"The list?"

"The list of things you need to do. You have me to drive you around, so move that off your list for now."

"Yes, but you won't be around for long."

"You worry a lot."

"Can you blame me?" Zoe asked, incredulous.

"I've upset you again."

"No, yes, maybe. It's this feeling of helplessness that's got me tied into knots."

"What can you do right now?"

"Figure out who to talk to at the community center."

"Finish your burger. That's what you can do."

"Jack—"

"Staying present and grounding yourself is a tool that can manage anxiety."

She leaned back in the plastic booth. "That's what I tell my clients. Yet I totally forget to take my own advice."

"We rarely listen to ourselves."

"You should be the counselor," she said.

"I'm too blunt."

"Sometimes that's what's needed."

"But mostly kids need to be listened to. I'm not a good listener."

She started to disagree but held her tongue. It was interesting how Jack saw himself versus how Zoe saw him.

"Do you need more ketchup?" he asked.

"No, I'm good." She finished her burger and sipped her lemonade.

A few minutes later they were in his truck headed for the community center. She noticed how he continually scanned his rearview and side mirrors, as if expecting trouble.

She made a plan in her mind about who she'd talk to and what she'd say.

How has Shannon been acting lately?

Did she seem upset or worried?

She'd start there and see if those questions opened any doors.

They entered the front of the center and checked in with the receptionist. Zoe noted that the building was previously a school that had been freshened up with a coat of paint and colorful posters on the walls.

A few minutes later a woman in her sixties joined them. She was dressed professionally in dark slacks and a burgundy sweater.

"Hello," she greeted. "I'm Wendy Yost, director of the community center."

"Nice to meet you." Zoe shook her hand. "I'm Zoe Pratt and this is Jack Monroe."

Wendy eyed Jack. "Jack Monroe from Search and Rescue?"

"Yes," Jack said.

"Oh, it's very good to meet you. We all appreciate everything you've done."

"You're welcome," he said, his voice flat.

"As I explained on the phone, I'm good friends with Shannon Banks," Zoe said.

"Shannon was such a wonderful young woman," Wendy said.

"She still is," Zoe blurted out.

"We're still searching for her," Jack added. "She has not been found."

"Oh, that *is* good news."

"Anyway, I was hoping you could answer some questions about Shannon?" Zoe said.

"Of course. Let's go to my office."

They headed down the hall and Wendy motioned to various rooms as they passed, explaining what they were used for: an exercise room, a mom and tots room, a club room where everyone from knitters to water color artists gathered.

"We serve residents of Skagit County, from children to retirees. Shannon mostly worked with kids on Tuesdays and Fridays from 6:00 to 9:00 p.m."

"You mean Angie's Youth Club?" Zoe asked.

"Yes, renamed after teenager Angie Adams." Wendy glanced at Jack.

"She died," Jack added.

Zoe sensed the subject disturbed him, so she redirected the conversation. "What types of things did Shannon do for Angie's Youth Club?"

"She created the program by developing activities and field trips to local businesses. She even worked with Sergeant Peterson to coordinate a few ride-alongs."

"I'll bet the kids loved that," Zoe said.

"They did. Shannon also taught kids how to set goals in her life skills workshop, and had a friend assist with a computer workshop."

"I have a right to be here!" a young voice echoed from around the corner.

Wendy picked up her pace, a worried expression creasing her brow.

"I'm sorry but you need to leave," an older, male voice said.

Wendy, Zoe and Jack turned the corner and saw an elderly gentleman trying to escort a teenager out of a classroom. The teenage girl had jet-black hair with streaks of dark red, and wore a torn denim jacket. Her face was flushed pink.

"I want to see Shannon!" the teen shouted.

"Hey, I'm Shannon's friend," Zoe said. "Can I help?"

Wendy motioned for the elderly man to step back.

"I have to talk to Shannon," the girl said.

"Well," Zoe began cautiously, "we don't know where Shannon is right now. We're all worried about her. I'm sure she'd want me to help. You seem very upset."

"She thinks I'm a loser, but I'm not!" the girl shouted.

"I doubt Shannon would think that you're a loser," Zoe tried.

"She kicked me out of Angie's Club. She hates me."

"She asked you to take a break and return when you could control your disrespectful attitude," Wendy offered.

"No, she kicked me out, I'll never be allowed back," the girl said.

"I'm sure we can figure this out," Zoe went on, trying to de-escalate the situation.

"I miss my friends." The teen's voice hitched.

"I would, too. I'm Zoe. What's your name?"

"Jeanie." She eyed Jack. "Who's he? A cop? Are you here to arrest me, cop?"

"He's my friend Jack."

"Your friend." Jeanie clenched her jaw as if she didn't believe Zoe.

"Yes. We sincerely want to help, Jeanie," Zoe promised.

"Then take this." Jeanie extended her arm, a piece of paper clutched between her fingers.

The elderly man took a step toward her.

"No, not you." She nodded at Jack. "The cop."

"I'm not a cop."

"Whatever." She waved the piece of paper.

Something felt off.

"This is proof I belong here," Jeanie said.

Jack took a few steps toward her.

"Jack, wait," Zoe said.

He froze, his back to Zoe, and raised his hands.

"Jack?" Zoe said.

He turned around with a defeated look on his face. Jeanie stepped slightly to her left so Zoe could see her clutching a gun.

SEVEN

Jack took a slow, deep breath. Calculated his options. The possibility of Zoe being shot outweighed any benefit of trying to disarm the teenager. He was stuck, because he hadn't read a signal, hadn't seen the signs that the girl intended violence.

Zoe must have because she told him to wait at the very moment the teen pulled the gun. She'd known something was about to happen.

"I'm going to sit down." Zoe went to a nearby table, her hands also up and visible.

"Get out of here, Zoe." The words escaped his lips before he even realized he'd spoken.

"No, I want her to stay. But they can go." Jeanie nodded at Wendy and the older man. They backed out of the room.

"Put the gun down," Jack tried.

"Shut up, cop."

There was no reasoning with this kid. She'd decided Jack was a police officer, the enemy, and only wanted to do her harm. If he tried to disarm her, the slightest miscalculation could end up in disaster.

"Come on, sit down," Zoe said, motioning to a nearby table.

The girl pressed the gun barrel into Jack's back. "You first."

Jack slowly sat at the table, unable to make eye contact with Zoe. Instead he focused on a poster across the room. It showed a mountain range and the words imprinted across the top read, Faith Can Move Mountains.

Faith. Too bad Jack didn't know how to access faith in a higher power. He could use some divine assistance right about now.

He noticed the girl had yet to sit down at the table, but Zoe and Jack were both seated, which put Jeanie in a position of control.

This was even worse than when Jack had stood as a barrier between the gun and Zoe. There had to be a safe solution. He considered everything from the position of the chairs around him to using the table as cover.

"You seem incredibly frustrated, Jeanie," Zoe said. "How can I help?"

What an odd question, Jack thought.

Jeanie didn't answer. Out of the corner of his eye, Jack saw her step closer to Zoe.

"Talk to me." Zoe touched the table beside her.

No, he didn't want the girl getting too close to Zoe.

As he was about to stand up and block Jeanie's aim toward Zoe, the girl started to back away toward the door. Good. He hoped she'd flee the scene and no one would get hurt.

"Come on, Jeanie. I seriously want to help," Zoe pushed.

"Then find Shannon," Jeanie said.

"We're trying, believe me," Zoe said. "But the weather is preventing Search and Rescue from going up into the mountains to look for her."

"You have to find her. She's the only one who can get me back into Angie's Club."

"You've got bigger problems than your social life."

"Jack," Zoe admonished.

Shame coursed through him as he shot a glance at Zoe. He'd never seen that look before. He snapped his attention to the Faith poster.

"Jeanie, please excuse my friend," Zoe said.

"What a jerk."

"He doesn't mean to be. Talk to me about the situation with Shannon."

"She cut me off and turned me away. This was the only place where people accepted me. It was bad enough when she stopped giving me the stuff for my dad, but then she said I couldn't come back because I was a danger to other kids. I'm the danger when she's dealing drugs?"

Jack snapped his attention from the poster to Zoe. No visible reaction. Then he saw her eyes blink three times rapidly. Blink, blink, blink. Pause. Blink, blink, blink. He wished he knew what she was thinking.

"I didn't know she was dealing drugs," Zoe said.

"Guess you weren't that great of friends, then," Jeanie said.

Zoe sighed. "Please know, I am sorry for your pain."

"Dad's the one in pain. That's why he needed the drugs. On Fridays I'd leave cash beneath the bear statue out back and she'd put drugs in my backpack. Then one Friday, nothing. We paid her and everything. When I asked her about it, she acted like she didn't know what I was talking about. We got into this huge argument and she kicked me out of the club."

"You didn't exchange money for drugs in person?" Zoe asked.

"We're not stupid, duh."

"Then how do you know it was Shannon?"

"She left a note with the first bottle of pills. It said she's got something for my dad, but it's not free."

Sirens echoed through the window.

"Oh no, they called police. I'm outta here."

"Jeanie—"

"Forget it." She turned and ran down the hall.

Jack stood to follow her and glanced at Zoe, though he wasn't sure why.

"Go," she said. "Don't get shot."

Jack cautiously followed the teenager. He spotted her at the end of the hall by an exit door. She paused, put the gun in a garbage can and took off outside. Why dump the gun?

Jack went after her, hesitating at the door in case

she was waiting for him with another weapon. He wouldn't be caught unawares again.

He cracked the door open and leaned back, out of range. Nothing.

He peered around the corner into the recreation area. Didn't see anyone. Jeanie had essentially disappeared.

Something was incredibly wrong. As Zoe waited for Jack to return, she tried making sense of what the teenager had said.

Shannon was a drug dealer.

Nope, did not make sense. Not even a little bit. Zoe wouldn't accept it.

Wendy poked her head into the room. "Police should arrive any minute."

"Great, thanks. How did you know it was safe to come back here?"

Wendy pointed to a camera in the room. "Some have cameras, some don't. I saw her leave."

Zoe nodded. "Did you hear what she said, too?"

"No, why?"

"She claims Shannon's been dealing drugs."

"I'll never believe that. Jeanie's trouble and Shannon knew it. She wanted her to get help and not be a bad influence on the other kids."

Zoe stood from the table, suddenly needing to feel taller, in control. The truth was, she felt totally out of control, like she'd been sucked into a tornado barreling across the countryside.

Jack returned with a strange look on his face.

"What?" she asked.

"She dumped the gun in the garbage can, then disappeared."

"Okay, good."

"Why is that good?"

"I didn't want to see her hurt during a shoot-out."

"She tried to kill me—you—us," Jack said. His tone sounded nothing short of judgmental.

"Did she?" Zoe said. "I think she was scared, angry and utterly frustrated."

"You've been scared and frustrated and haven't threatened to kill anyone," he said.

"I'll go greet deputies when they arrive." Wendy excused herself, probably wanting to get away from the tension bouncing back and forth between Jack and Zoe.

"You knew, didn't you, that she planned to do us harm?" Jack asked.

"I sensed something, yes. But the more I spoke with her, the more I realized it was about her pain, not her wanting to inflict pain on others."

"I don't understand how you came to that conclusion."

"No, you wouldn't." She glanced at him, realizing she needed to clarify her statement or else he'd take it the wrong way. "I have a master's degree in counseling, plus five years' experience with this age group, remember?"

"I'm sorry about your friend."

"Whoa, signal before you change lanes next time."

"Okay. I'll try."

She would've chuckled at the fact he was playing along with the banter, but she was too distraught about Shannon to find anything funny.

Especially because Jeanie had accused Shan of dealing drugs.

"That's wrong," Jack said.

"What?"

"I said that wrong. I meant, I'm sorry you had to find out that way, about your friend dealing drugs."

"I'm not accepting it yet, so let's drop the subject."

"The sheriff's office will ask us what Jeanie said."

"I know."

"We'll have to tell them the truth."

"Yes, we will. That still doesn't make Shannon a drug dealer."

Jack headed back to the suite where Zoe would pick up what she'd purchased this morning, and then he'd take her to the Ashford Inn.

So much for proving Shannon's innocence, Zoe thought. Her statement to Detective Perry seemed to solidify his suspicion that Shannon was a criminal.

Zoe wished she could speak with Jeanie again, but it seemed that she had run away. Detective Perry sent a deputy to Jeanie's house, but she had not returned.

Detective Perry. Zoe could hardly look at him when she'd repeated what the girl had said: *I'm the danger when she's dealing drugs?*

No, Zoe wouldn't believe it. There had to be another explanation.

"They issued a BOLO for Jeanie, so they'll find her," Jack said.

Again, it amazed Zoe how he sensed what she was thinking about. "Let's hope they're kind to her when they do."

"You'll have to explain that to me some time," he said.

"Explain what?"

"How you can be so forgiving to someone who threatened you and accused your friend of being a drug dealer."

She glanced out the window. "It's called giving someone grace."

"It's foreign to me."

"You're not alone." She remembered the last argument she and Tim had before their breakup. Their challenges weren't solely caused by his need to climb the corporate ladder. No, Tim had lacked the ability or at least the interest to learn to offer grace. The implosion of their relationship taught her it would be easier if she found someone who shared her values, including her faith. It also taught her how blind she could be when she loved someone, blind enough to look past their faults.

Like she had with Shannon?

Was that what was happening with her best friend?

This was different. She knew Shannon, her family, her upbringing. Zoe would not accept that Shannon had changed so much in the past ten years.

Then again, Tim seemed to change in the fourteen months they'd dated, from generous dating partner to self-absorbed jerk, and Zoe hadn't even seen it happen.

"You need to love Jesus to do that, right? To give grace?" Jack said.

His comment snapped her out of her analysis.

"I don't even know Jesus," he said.

"Well, you're more like Him than you think."

"Why do you say that?"

"You volunteer to save people's lives. That's pretty selfless."

His eyebrows furrowed, like before when he was processing something.

"Can I ask you a question?" she said.

He nodded.

"Angie Adams…?"

His grip tightened on the steering wheel.

"I'm sorry," Zoe backtracked. "Never mind."

"She died."

"I know."

"She didn't have to die."

"That's…sad. How did—"

"She made a foolish choice to go into the mountains during a snowstorm with her friends."

Zoe waited, thinking he had more to say.

"Those weren't friends. Friends would have stayed with her after she fell."

"And they didn't?"

"No, they were worried about getting into trouble. Only after they came down off the mountain did they call Emergency, made up a story about Angie going up there alone. By the time we found her…" His voice trailed off as he pulled into the motel parking lot.

"She was gone?"

Jack didn't look at her, just stared straight ahead at their motel room door. "Not quite. But she did eventually die." He pinned her with dark blue eyes. "Because I couldn't save her."

Zoe opened her mouth to correct him, to say it wasn't his fault, that he wasn't a doctor, nor did he make the unwise decision to hike in a snowstorm or choose friends who would abandon him.

But she recognized the look on his face: a look of self-defeat and guilt that couldn't be eased with platitudes from a stranger. And in his eyes, Zoe was still a stranger he'd known only a couple of days, a stranger who had no right to tell him how he should feel.

Zoe didn't have any right to insinuate herself in his feelings, his life.

"You're not talking," Jack said.

"No, I'm holding space."

He looked at her hands.

"It's another term for compassionate listening."

"The purpose of which is…?"

"To support you, to sit with your pain."

"That's pointless." He opened his door.

She grabbed his arm. He froze and looked at her.

"I'm sorry you weren't able to save Angie."

"I need to check on Romeo."

She released him and watched as he walked to the motel room and opened the door. The dog practically jumped into his arms, easing the strained expression pinching at the corners of Jack's eyes. He didn't know how to deal with emotions like guilt, and she didn't want to "shrink" him, an expression used by some of her friends when she offered advice. In this case she had no advice or wisdom to give a man who obviously held himself accountable for a young woman's death.

He was brave indeed to feel such guilt, yet still search for lost or injured hikers. For some, the loss of one life would be enough to walk away.

She grabbed her shoulder bag, got out of his truck and went into their room at the lodge. Romeo greeted her with a perfect sit.

"Good boy," Jack said, then looked at Zoe. "I got a text from SAR. There's a break in the weather and Command wants to send teams up."

"Go, go," she said.

"You'll stay here?"

"I'll call a cab to take me to the inn."

"No, I'll take you."

"I don't want you to waste time."

"It's on the way."

Zoe quickly gathered her shopping bags and they were back in the truck within minutes, headed for the Ashford Inn.

"You didn't tell anyone where you'd be staying, correct?" he said.

"Other than police and you? No."

"Good."

"You still think I'm in danger?"

"You're vulnerable if you're alone. At least at the inn you'll be with other people. The innkeeper seems strict about not giving out information regarding her guests."

"You know her?"

"No, I tried to find out if you'd checked in yesterday and she wouldn't confirm or deny."

"So that's good."

"Yes. You should be safe there. I did a background check on the owners. They are solid people."

"Wow, thanks."

"I can call the sheriff's office and see if Sergeant Peterson can park a patrol car out front or at least check on you tonight. I'm not sure how long I'm going to be gone. It could be hours, or if the weather holds, days."

"No problem. I've really appreciated your support." And she did, but she realized she was growing more dependent on him than she should. This man had a life and, at present, a critical mission.

She needed him to find Shannon.

Two hours later Jack and his team approached the location where a ranger said he'd spotted a woman in an orange ski jacket running through the snow shouting. The ranger wasn't close enough to assist, so he'd called it in. Jack hadn't told Zoe the part about the woman shouting for help because he didn't want to upset her.

If the woman was Shannon, that meant she had escaped her captors, which would explain why the man who'd broken into her home the other night and assaulted Zoe asked where "she" was.

The kidnapper had lost his hostage.

Yet Shannon had been unable to find her way to safety or call for assistance. That puzzled Jack. Perhaps she didn't want to return home, fearing the repercussions of her drug dealing activity?

He'd never forget the look on Zoe's face when Jeanie dropped that bomb. It was like Zoe hadn't understood what the girl was saying, that the prospect of Shannon dealing drugs was completely nonsensical.

A lot of things seemed nonsensical to Jack these past forty-eight hours, the least of which were Zoe's inconsistent reactions.

A young woman threatens her; she forgives her.

Jack confesses his worst failure; she "holds space" for him.

And then there was her question about Jack missing SAR once he sold his company and went traveling.

His plan had always been to conquer one goal and move on to the next. Develop a successful company and sell it. Go traveling and explore places he'd never been. It seemed like a worthwhile plan.

Zoe's comment about missing SAR bothered him. He hadn't considered the human element in his plans. He never had to consider anyone else but himself. So why did her comment set his mind spinning like a hard drive gone bad?

He embraced order and sense, something not often found in relationships. He puzzled over his new acquaintance, Zoe Pratt, especially the fact that he liked being around her. Perhaps a good reason to distance himself. Being fascinated by something he didn't understand didn't mean he had to embrace it.

Overthinking again.

"I think I see tracks up ahead," Sally said.

Command had assembled two teams. Jack had been paired with Sally and her dog, Butch, plus Deputies Hauf and Ortman, who had hiking and even climbing experience. The second team was approaching from the north end of the red zone, as they'd named it.

Hauf and Ortman scanned their surroundings for anything suspicious, while Sally, Jack and their dogs focused on tracking the missing woman.

Romeo stopped and stuck his nose in the air. At least this area was relatively flat, and Jack wouldn't have to worry about Romeo sliding over the edge of a cliff.

His dog took off, and Butch joined in, the dogs racing up ahead and out of sight.

"Where'd they go?" Deputy Hauf said.

"They'll be back."

Jack picked up his pace, but Romeo didn't return to pull at the toggle at Jack's belt. Neither did Butch. Jack and Sally shared a look, not sure what to make of the unusual behavior.

"What?" Deputy Hauf said.

"Something's not—"

The crack of a gunshot echoed across the canyon.

EIGHT

The deputies and Sally hit the ground.

Jack took off, the only thought in his head that he had get to Romeo. The dog had been a stabilizing force in his life, a good friend. A searing pain slashed through his chest to think Romeo had been hurt by a coward with a gun.

"Get down!" one of the deputies called after him.

Jack's leg muscles burned as he raced through the snow in almost slow motion, fighting the heaviness as it collected on his boots. He reached a sharp turn and didn't even hesitate to forge ahead around the blind corner.

Another shot rang out. Was it close? Far away? There was no way to know due to the vastness of the mountains and their echoes. Jack choose to ignore the threat.

A third shot. This one hit a boulder not twenty feet from Jack's position.

He had to get to—

Romeo sprang from the nearby forest and dove at Jack. Jack caught him and went down, scrambling behind the boulder for cover.

"You okay, buddy?"

The dog whined and released a few yelps. Jack ripped off his gloves with his teeth and ran his hands over the dog's fur. No blood. He breathed a sigh of relief.

Barking echoed in the distance. Butch was still out there, and knowing that Lab's attitude, Butch was probably trying to disarm the shooter. This was one instance when Jack was appreciative of the Bernese blood running through Romeo's veins. Like his name, Romeo was a lover, not a fighter. Butch, on the other hand...

"Hey!" Sally said, coming around the back of the boulder.

The deputies were close behind. "I told you to stay back," Deputy Hauf said to both Jack and Sally.

"Our dogs are like an appendage, so save the lecture," Sally said, then looked at Jack. "Butch?"

"I hear him, but haven't seen him."

"He never knows when to back down, stupid dog," Sally said.

Jack sensed she used the word *stupid* because she was hurting for her dog, worried about his well-being.

"Try the whistle," Jack said.

With a nod, Sally pulled out the specialized whistle that only a dog could hear. She blew, and Romeo immediately started barking.

It took less than ten seconds and Butch came racing through the white snow toward the group. He rushed up to Sally and she hugged him.

"You stinker, stop picking fights." She looked at Jack and nodded her thanks.

"They found something that disturbed them," Jack said.

"Yeah, but we can't get to it," Sally said.

"Base, do you copy, over?" Deputy Hauf said into his radio.

"Go ahead, over."

"This is Deputy Hauf. We're taking fire, over."

"Can you retreat, over?"

"Questionable, over."

"We can assemble a backup team, but it might take a while to get to you, over."

"Roger that," Hauf said.

"We may not have a while," Deputy Ortman muttered, clutching his gun in his hand.

"They're awfully bold to be shooting at police," Hauf said.

"The kidnapper wants to get her back before we find her," Jack said.

"You think the dogs found her?" Ortman said.

"Doubtful, or they would have returned to us and pulled on the toggles," Jack said.

"What do you think?" Deputy Ortman said.

"We wait for backup," Hauf ordered.

Twenty-seven minutes later they got a call from base that they were sending backup, but it would take at least an hour.

The shooter had been quiet in those twenty-seven minutes, which made Jack wonder if he was still present.

"What should we do?" Ortman asked Deputy Hauf.

"Cover me."

"Wait, what—"

"Return fire if he shoots." Hauf got into a position and Ortman knelt beside him.

Hauf ran up the trail, dodging behind trees and snowdrifts to stay out of range.

No shots were fired.

It was a good assumption that the shooter had left the scene. He'd probably fled to avoid getting caught by police. But had he found Shannon Banks?

Hauf went higher, then disappeared out of sight. Deputy Ortman was still aiming his gun at the ridge above.

The buzz of silence was deafening.

Jack pulled out his binoculars and scrutinized the area where Deputy Hauf had disappeared. Had the shooter been quietly waiting for one of them to come looking for him?

Ortman's radio crackled with the sound of Hauf's voice.

"All clear. Get up here."

Jack spotted Deputy Hauf wave from the top of the ridge.

"You stay back," Ortman said to Jack and Sally.

As he climbed up the trail to join his partner,

Sally and Jack looked at each other. They shook their heads and followed the deputy. The dogs anticipated the plan and ran ahead of them, straight back to what had intrigued them before. Sally and Jack got to the top of the ridge and found the deputies standing over an odd site: an orange jacket stretched across a stick, almost like a scarecrow.

"What on earth is that?" Sally said.

"Perhaps Shannon's pumpkin coat," Jack offered. The deputies looked at him.

"Apparently she owns a jacket that color."

"What is this, some kind of game?" Deputy Hauf said.

"Looks like," Ortman said. "But why draw us out here?"

"It's a distraction," Jack said. It was the most logical explanation.

"And shooting at us?" Ortman said.

"To keep us engaged." The reality of what was happening flooded Jack's chest with dread.

"Because they didn't want us to find Shannon?" Sally asked.

"He went to a lot of trouble to bring us out here, why?" Deputy Ortman said.

"To keep us occupied because…" Jack hesitated. "Zoe." He motioned for Romeo and headed back to the trail.

"Where are you going?" Sally asked.

"Back to town. They're after Zoe Pratt."

Jack never should have left her alone.

* * *

Zoe spent a few hours at the inn reading Shannon's journal and making notes. She had a pretty good idea about what to do next, who to talk to. She'd continue speaking with work associates, then people from church.

She flopped back on the bed and sighed. *Please, Lord, let them find Shannon.*

As she lay there praying, trying to relax and get out of fight-or-flight mode, something Jeanie said popped into the forefront of her mind: *On Fridays I'd leave cash beneath the bear statue out back and she'd put drugs in my backpack.*

They'd made the exchange anonymously. Anyone could have been selling Jeanie drugs and claiming to be Shannon.

"I still don't believe it." Zoe sat up, determined. She needed to do something besides hide out in this room and pray.

But she didn't have her car, or know anyone who could drive her. Her driver was otherwise indisposed by his real work: finding Shannon.

Glancing at the clock, she realized it was nearly six. Marsha, the innkeeper, said she and her husband would put out light refreshments from four to six. Hopefully they hadn't been cleared away.

Zoe brushed her hair in the private bathroom, put on a fleece in case it was chilly downstairs and went in search of food.

A crackling fire warmed the main living area.

Beside the fireplace was a serving table with a pot of coffee, tea and snacks. She approached the table and her mouth watered at the sight of a cheese and fruit plate, scones and butter cookies.

"Hello?" she said, wanting to share her thanks. No one responded. She seemed to be completely alone.

When Zoe checked in, Marsha had said she might go out for supplies, but Zoe had hoped she'd be available for an afternoon chat. Zoe wouldn't mind the distraction of light conversation, otherwise she'd keep worrying about Jack, Shannon and the mission.

She poured tea into a purple-and-pink-floral china cup, put grapes and strawberries on a plate and plucked a scone from the serving tray.

As she took a bite of the scone, the lights went out, plunging her into darkness. She stifled a gasp.

They'd found her.

Instinct drove her to crouch behind a Queen Anne chair for cover, although it wouldn't take a rocket scientist to find her back there. Staying out of sight, she quietly set her plate and cup on the floor. She wished she had something with which to defend herself, but how could she have known going for snacks would put her in danger?

Then again, she should assume she was always in danger until they found Shannon.

The click of a door echoed from the kitchen.

She held her breath. *Don't make a sound.*

She carefully slipped off her shoes. Waited.

Floorboards creaked, announcing someone's presence. If it was one of the innkeepers, or even a guest, they'd speak out, right?

Creak, creak.

The sound moved from the back of the house to the front, toward the stairs.

She could hear soft footsteps climbing the stairs to the second floor. She glanced up at the ceiling.

The intruder was upstairs.

This was her chance.

She grabbed her shoes and tiptoed toward the back of the house, through the kitchen and out the door. She wished she had her jacket, but there was no time for that now. Slipping on her shoes, she eyed the surrounding property, looking for a spot to hide and call 911.

Thankfully the sidewalk out back had been cleared of snow. She rushed toward the garage and darted behind it, then peeked up at the house.

And saw a man in a black jacket pass by the window as he searched her room.

The journal. She'd left it upstairs.

She'd tucked it beneath the pillow, but if the guy tried hard enough, he'd find it.

The same man who'd kidnapped Shannon? But if Shan had escaped and search teams went to find her, why was this creep down below when he should be up in the mountains looking for her?

Because he was after Zoe.

He stepped into view as he passed by the window. Hugging herself against the chill, she squinted to see if it was the same guy who'd kidnapped Shan.

It wasn't.

It was the man who'd broken into Shannon's house that first night.

He peered out the window and she darted out of view. Had he seen her?

She turned and tore off, racing down the partially shoveled sidewalks toward a house with lights on. Surely someone would let her in. Then she considered how she appeared right now, terrified, without a jacket and probably wild-eyed. She needed to calm down before she knocked on a stranger's door asking for help.

Help. She hadn't called 911 yet. Needed to do that—

The sound of a door slamming shot fear down her spine. He'd seen her and was coming after her.

She ran faster, panic ringing in her ears. She got to the corner and turned, scanning the surrounding homes. Spotted one with Christmas lights still up, more than a month after the holiday.

A car engine started behind her. Was he going to run her down?

She glanced over her shoulder. The beam of headlights made her squint. Instinct drove her to veer right, up a sidewalk to the closest front door. But this house was dark. No one was home.

Heading toward the neighbor's yard, she stumbled through the juniper bushes. She'd make it to the house with the Christmas lights. She'd get help there, she'd—

A tall form stepped into her path up ahead. She spun around and ran back the other direction. There were two of them? Since she didn't have her purse, she didn't have the pepper spray.

She should've called 911. Now she was racing through the neighborhood, and no one knew where she was, no one would know what had happened to her.

"Stop." A hand gripped her shoulder.

She started swinging, fully expecting the assailant to grab her wrists or toss her over his shoulder.

"It's Jack."

She froze. Opened her eyes, and looked up into his handsome face, lit by the ambient glow of a streetlight.

"Come on," he said in a soft, gentle tone.

He took her hand, the contact warm and comforting. Jack led her toward an evergreen tree and they climbed beneath the apron for shelter.

From this vantage point, Zoe had a clear view of the street. An SUV cruised by, a piercing spotlight flickering as it pointed at the houses across the street.

"Shhh," Jack whispered, shielding her from view.

She realized his dark green jacket would blend

in with the trees, whereas she was wearing a light-colored fleece. She automatically leaned into him and focused on slow and steady breathing. *Inhale on the count of five, exhale on the count of five.*

As seconds stretched by, she realized Jack was holding her firmly against his chest.

Both she and Jack turned their heads away from view so their faces wouldn't be seen by the driver of the SUV. Maybe twenty or thirty seconds later Jack glanced up and so did she. The car was gone.

"Did you call 911?" he whispered.

She shook her head.

"Call them." He started to get up, but she couldn't let go of his jacket.

"Good idea. Here." He removed her grip, took off his jacket and placed it around her shoulders. "Got your phone?"

She nodded and pulled it out of her back pocket.

"Call 911."

"Okay."

But it wasn't okay. She didn't want him to leave her alone in the tree.

He started to get up and she gripped his sweater sleeve.

"I'll be right back," he said, and gave her hand a squeeze.

She released him, trusting his word. This was Jack Monroe, a man incapable of lying. A man who was honest to a fault. If he said he'd be back, then he would.

"Call." He nodded at the phone in her hand and climbed out from beneath the cover.

It took every ounce of self-control not to wrap his arms around Zoe again and stay hidden with her. The look of fear and vulnerability on her face struck something deep in his chest, something that argued staying with and protecting her was more important than getting the license plate and description of the SUV that was stalking her.

But in order to put an end to the danger constantly threatening her, Jack had to get more information. He would help authorities identify the assailant that had nearly taken Zoe.

Because Jack hadn't been there to protect her.

He rushed down a driveway to the street in time to see taillights disappear around a corner. Gone. Jack had nothing but a vague description of a tan-colored SUV. He turned to go back to Zoe and found himself facing off with a middle-aged man with a beard.

Pointing a rifle at Jack's chest.

Jack raised his hands, a myriad of thoughts racing through his brain.

Stay hidden, Zoe.

What an idiot to expose myself like this.

Is this guy just going to keep me here while his partner pulls around in the SUV?

"Hands behind your head," the bearded guy ordered.

Jack did as he was told, having calculated the kind of damage a rifle like that could do to a human being. Where were the police? Surely Zoe had called them.

Unless she'd been too traumatized to accurately describe their location.

"Now turn around," the guy demanded.

Not good. The only reason to turn around was to make shooting Jack an easier task.

"What's this about?" Jack said, trying to buy time.

"Where is the woman?"

"I don't know." If he charged the guy, Jack was dead. He needed to buy enough time for the sheriff's deputies to arrive.

"Who are you?" Jack asked.

The guy motioned with the rifle. "On your knees, hotshot."

If there *was* a God, Jack hoped—no, he prayed—that Zoe was still hidden beneath the evergreen and wasn't watching this.

He slowly lowered himself to his knees, calculating an angle at which he could attack without being shot squarely in the chest.

The sound of muted sirens echoed in the distance. Zoe had made the call. Jack just needed a few seconds. Five, four…

"You sure you want to do this?" Jack said, his knees wet from the snow.

Calculations were done. He knew the correct angle that would cause the least amount of damage.

Three, two…

"You talk a lot."

One.

Jack charged.

The gun went off.

Something smashed against Jack's head.

A woman screamed. Zoe?

Jack went facedown in the snow, his last thought that the guy's accomplice had Zoe.

NINE

"The street behind the Ashford Inn, I don't know the name," Zoe said to the 911 operator. She peered through the tree branches, needles scratching her cheek, to see what was going on out front.

Was that…?

"No," she gasped.

"Ma'am, what is it?" the operator asked.

Jack was on his knees, his hands interlaced behind his head. Facing a man with a long rifle.

Zoe was about to scream, when Jack charged the gunman. They stumbled out of view and a gunshot rang out. Zoe shoved branches aside to get a better look.

Jack was down, motionless in the snow. And the shooter was standing over him.

"He's going to kill Jack."

"Ma'am—"

She bolted out of the cover.

Don't be stupid. Don't sacrifice yourself, because then Jack's death won't count for—

His death? No, she wouldn't let that happen.

She was smart. As a kid, she'd outwitted a rare genetic disease. She could certainly figure out a way to save Jack.

"How close are deputies?" she said into the phone.

"Four, maybe five minutes away."

"I'm going to distract him."

"Ma'am, I have to advise you—"

She pocketed the phone and took off through a backyard, still out of view, screaming at the top of her lungs. She hoped to both lure the shooter away from Jack's defenseless body and get some Neighborhood Watch action going. The more people who came out to see what was going on, the less likely the guy would commit murder on someone's front lawn.

She heard a door open at a neighboring house. Good, people were paying attention. As she crossed through another backyard, she came face-to-face with the shooter. "Don't shoot, please don't shoot!" She put her hands together and prayed.

"I'm not going to shoot you," the man said.

Of course not. He wanted to kidnap her.

She kept praying, prayed that the police would arrive, prayed that Jack would be okay, even if she was taken on his watch.

"Ma'am, are you okay?"

Her eyes popped open.

"Am I okay? What an odd question coming from the guy who's trying to kidnap me and beat up an innocent man."

"That man out front? I don't know how you can call him innocent, considering he was chasing you through the neighborhood. That's why I came out here in the first place. And I certainly have no interest in kidnapping you."

"Oh, right," Zoe said. From an innocent bystander's perspective, Jack had been chasing her, even though he'd been trying to protect and defend her. To this bearded guy, it probably looked like Jack was the perpetrator.

"There's been a misunderstanding," she said, walking toward the front where Jack had been assaulted. "The man out front is actually with Search and Rescue. He protected me from an attacker."

The bearded guy shook his head in frustration. "Why didn't he say so?"

"Well, in his defense, he probably assumed you were the bad guy. But you are…?" she prompted.

"Billy Arndt. I live across the street." He pointed to a brick bungalow where a dog was barking insistently from the window. "My dog, Tank, knew something was up. When I checked the window, I saw you running from that guy and figured I'd assist. I called 911."

"So did I. How badly is my friend hurt?"

"He'll probably have a headache for a few hours. He came at me and I had to defend myself. I'm sorry about that."

"I understand."

"He could have told me who he was."

"Did you identify yourself as a concerned neighbor?"

"No." He glanced at Zoe. "Point taken."

When they reached the front of the house, the sound of sirens grew louder. She went to Jack, who lay on the ground, and she knelt in the snow beside him.

"Jack?" She willed his blue eyes to open. She placed her palm against his cheek in the hopes the connection would bring him back to consciousness. "It's okay," she said. "We're safe."

He blinked his eyes open. She offered an encouraging nod. Then he glanced over her shoulder, and his jaw clenched.

"He's not one of them," she said. "He's a neighbor, Billy Arndt. He was trying to help."

Jack glanced back at Zoe, as if trying to reconcile her words with what had happened to him. "He threatened to kill me."

"I was trying to hold you for police," Billy said. "I didn't know you were friends with the young lady. I'm sorry."

She took off Jack's jacket.

"No," Jack said. "You need it."

"I'm not soaked in snow." She started to lay it across him. Jack sat up, gripping his head.

Two squad cars and a dark sedan pulled up to the curb. Billy laid his rifle on the ground. Detective Perry got out of the sedan and approached Zoe and Jack.

"Did the kidnapper assault him?" Perry asked.

"I assaulted him by accident," Billy said. "I thought he was the bad guy."

Two deputies joined them. A few front doors opened, and neighbors peeked out to get a look.

"What happened?" Detective Perry asked Zoe.

"The lights went out at the Ashford Inn and I feared they'd found me, so I took off."

"I saw her running away and followed," Jack said. "I saw another guy, over six feet tall, in pursuit so I strategized a way to assist without revealing my presence."

"At least not to humans," Billy interjected. Perry glanced at him. "My dog alerted me that something was going on outside and I saw the young woman tearing through the neighborhood like a cougar was on her heels. I got my weapon and went to investigate. That's when I ran into this guy." He nodded at Jack.

"They both mistook the other for the guy who was after me," Zoe said.

"Everything okay, officer?" a woman called from her front porch across the street.

"Yes, ma'am, please go back into your house," one of the deputies said.

"Did you get a look at him?" Detective Perry asked Zoe.

"The man in my room was the intruder from the other night."

"He drove a newer model SUV, tan, with some kind of rack on top," Jack offered.

"Plate number?" Perry asked.

"Too far away. It had a spotlight on the side, like you have on squad cars."

Detective Perry glanced at the deputy on his right. "Question the neighbors. Maybe they saw something." He nodded at the other deputy. "Head back to the Ashford Inn and locate the innkeepers. Radio me when it's safe and we'll take her back to get her things."

"After I go to the urgent care with Jack," Zoe said.

"I don't need urgent care," Jack said.

"To check out your head injury?"

"I'm fine." He stood to prove it and winced only slightly. "Where are you going to move her?"

"Not sure yet," Perry said. "But wherever it is, no one can know the location, not even you."

Of course the detective was leaving Jack out of the loop, because Jack had utterly failed. He could have gotten the plate number, or some other detail about the car that would help authorities find the intruder and unravel this mess, but he hadn't. Instead, Jack ended up in the snow, threatened by a well-meaning neighbor.

Maybe if his social acumen had been more sound, he would have asked the right questions to decipher that Billy wasn't the perpetrator. Instead, he'd missed an opportunity to develop a lead in the case.

And Zoe was still in danger.

Jack and Zoe waited in the back of Deputy Perry's sedan for the all clear to return to the inn and gather her things. Then she'd disappear. Jack would never see her again, at least not while this was an open investigation.

"I won't agree to it, by the way," Zoe said.

"Agree to what?"

"Shutting you out. I don't care what police say, you know details of this case better than anyone and I have confidence you're the one person who can keep me safe." She hesitated. "Unless you need to get back to your business. I would totally understand if you—"

"I didn't keep you safe today."

"Uh, yeah, you did."

"I ended up facedown in the snow."

"You hid me from the guy chasing me."

"The friendly neighbor could have been one of them."

"But he wasn't."

"I shouldn't have gone on the search mission."

"Whoa, you forgot to signal again."

"I can't protect you if I'm not here."

"I appreciate that, but you're not the only one with the goal of protecting me. I have a whole police department on my side, remember?"

"I don't like Detective Perry."

"You don't have to like him. As long as he does his job and solves this case. Anyway, I won't agree to their plan of whisking me off to some secret location without you knowing where I am."

"You may not have a choice."

"We always have a choice. That's the beauty of living."

He studied Zoe, an adorable woman who had been threatened more times in the past two days than most people were in an entire lifetime.

"Is it your faith that makes you so strong?" he said.

"Partially. And life experience."

He waited, hoping she'd share more.

"My little brother was very sick growing up. They told us he may not make it, but I wouldn't accept that. I researched the condition, encouraged my parents to ask the right questions, and basically took over running the household. But there was no one to take care of me. Then Shannon's family treated me like one of their own, including taking me to church with them. Life isn't easy, but it's exciting, that's for sure."

"You were so upset when we were under the tree."

"Me and adrenaline, not a good mix. I kind of fall apart, sorry."

"I liked it, I mean, that I could make you feel safe."

"Me, too." She smiled.

Did his heart skip a beat? That's what it felt like.

"That's one reason I need you around," she said. "The fact you make me feel safe."

"There are other reasons?" He could feel his pulse quicken.

"Shannon is not a drug dealer and I need to prove it. You know how the community center has a video feed?"

"Yes."

"Jeanie said she never got the drugs directly from Shannon, but they mysteriously appeared in her backpack. What if we accessed the center's video feed, went back a few weeks and looked for whoever put the drugs in Jeanie's backpack?"

His heart sank. Zoe wanted his tech skills more than anything else. He sighed.

"What, is accessing the video feed against the law or something?"

"I'm sure if we asked nicely, they'll let us take a look."

"But?"

But I was hoping you wanted me around because you liked me, that you were feeling this intense pull between us, too.

"It's a long shot. They may not keep weeks of video," he said, noting her hopeful expression. "But it's worth a try." He glanced out the opposite window, suddenly needing distance and fresh air to recalibrate his mind. "I'm going to check on the status of things."

As he got out of the car, she touched his arm. "What did I say?"

He glanced back at her concerned face.

"I upset you," she said.

Jack managed to hide his immediate reaction, which was to affirm that she had, in fact, hurt his feelings. What good would it do to admit the truth? She wanted his assistance to find her friend, that was all. There was nothing more going on here, at least on her end.

"I'm worried about your safety," he said.

"Are you sure it's not something else? I mean, besides that?"

Detective Perry stepped up to the car to address them both. "It's safe to go back to the inn and get your things. We located the innkeeper, who was asleep in her suite downstairs. We're considering the possibility someone drugged her tea."

"You mean the tea that was out in the living room?" Zoe asked.

"Yes. Why, did you drink it?"

"I didn't have time. A good thing, I guess."

"How did they know where Zoe was staying?" Jack asked. "I called the inn and they wouldn't confirm or deny her presence."

"Don't have an answer on that yet. Deputy Ortman will drive you to the inn, then we'll move you to a secure location."

"With Jack."

"Excuse me?"

"He needs to be a part of this."

"*He* is a search-and-rescue volunteer, not a police officer."

"He is also a friend and I need his support."

The next morning Zoe awoke with a gasp from a fitful night's sleep. She sat up and scanned her surroundings, remembering where she was and why.

Someone had discovered her location at the inn. Police had whisked her away to a motor lodge outside of town and Perry had reserved a suite under a false name to protect her identity.

She was in a bedroom, under the covers, with her clothes on. Alone.

"Jack," she whispered.

She didn't like the fact that her first thought upon waking was of him. She should be focused on finding answers to Shannon's crisis.

But Jack was on her mind. Had she thanked him appropriately for saving her last night? For pulling her under the tree for cover and holding her until the threat had passed?

She shared her gratitude with the Lord that she'd been able to convince Detective Perry she needed Jack in her life. Hopefully he was in the next room.

She washed her face and brushed her teeth, thanks to supplies she'd picked up yesterday. She opened the door to the main living area, complete with kitchenette. It was empty.

She wandered to the front window and pushed aside the curtain, spotted a squad car out front, plus Jack's SUV. The front door opened and Romeo raced inside.

"Hey, I missed you." Zoe reached down to pet the dog's fur.

"Got us some breakfast," Jack said, carrying a brown take-out bag to the kitchen table.

Deputy Ortman poked his head into the suite. "Everything good?" he asked Zoe.

"Yes, thank you."

He closed the door and Zoe joined Jack at the kitchen table. "Any news?"

"Yes, actually, some good news."

She held her breath. *Shannon.*

"Sorry, not about your friend."

She sighed.

"They found the suspect, the man they think was after you last night. His vehicle fits the description, including the floodlight. They have him in custody, but he's not speaking until his lawyer arrives. They're doing a background check. Detective Perry wants you to come to the station to identify him."

"Oh, okay. I can go right now." She stood.

"Not yet. Detective Perry will notify us when he needs us. In the meantime, we stay here."

She sat back down. "You never told me about the mission yesterday."

Jack pulled out a foam container and placed it in front of her. "Egg sandwiches."

"Thanks. The search-and-rescue call?"

"A park ranger radioed in that he saw a woman in an orange jacket."

"Shannon?" Zoe said, hope filling her chest. Then again, if anything good had come from the search, Jack would have told her already.

"Maybe Shannon," he said. "We don't know for sure who it was."

"An orange jacket, it had to be her. What was she doing? Did she look okay? Was she hurt?"

He didn't answer right away. Instead, he meticulously opened his breakfast sandwich container. She sensed he didn't want to answer.

"You didn't find her…body, did you?"

He snapped his attention to her. "No, why?"

"You're stalling. That means you don't want to tell me something. As long as you didn't find my friend's dead body, I can handle whatever you've got. Come on, what happened?"

"It doesn't matter, we didn't find her."

"What aren't you telling me?"

He glanced at Romeo, who lay next to him on the floor. "Someone shot at us."

"At the dog?"

"Sounded like it. Romeo was way ahead of us and we heard shots. But he's okay, aren't ya, buddy?" His tone seemed lighter than she'd heard before.

Romeo wagged his tail, excited about Jack's attention.

"I think it was a diversion, a way to keep law enforcement occupied while they came for you again."

"Wow."

"I've contacted the community center and they're fine with us looking through video feed. They keep twenty-one days at a time, so there's a chance we'll see the drug exchange."

"It's not Shannon."

"You should eat your sandwich and raise your blood sugar so we can work."

"Okay, Doctor Jack."

She thought a slight smile curved the corner of his lips, but couldn't be sure.

As they ate, Zoe mused how comfortable it was to share a meal with this unusual man. The silence between them was pleasant, not stressful. She didn't feel silently judged like when her ex would take her to a fancy restaurant and then wrinkle his nose when she chose to order French fries instead of rice as her side dish with salmon. It was like Tim was always worried about impressing people around him, whereas Zoe's priority was feeling at ease and comfortable in her environment.

She'd grown up walking on eggshells, never

knowing when an argument would be triggered by financial strain or a medical diagnosis. Her parents and Zoe were stressed out because they loved Ryan so much and didn't want to lose him. But even after he recovered, the family didn't seem to heal. The stress had taken its toll, and her parents had never been the same.

Shannon's family had always been there for her.

"The video feed," Zoe said. "Can we go back to the community center and take a look after we stop by the sheriff's office?"

"We don't have to go to the community center. I received permission to access their server, so we can do that now."

Zoe nodded. She was both anxious to prove her friend's innocence and nervous about the possibility she was a drug dealer.

"Unless you want to wait?" Jack offered.

"No, let's do it." Zoe moved her chair to sit beside him, and he opened his laptop. After a few minutes, he had access to the community center's video. They focused on the hours Shan volunteered for Angie's Youth Club.

"Jeanie said the drugs appeared in her backpack on Fridays," Zoe said.

Jack fast-forwarded to the appropriate date. The first Friday they watched showed nothing, at least nothing featuring Shannon Banks.

"Maybe I'm being unrealistic," Zoe said.

"Hang on, let me see if I can find another camera." Jack tapped at the keyboard. A few seconds later another shot appeared, this one focused on the entry to the building. Teens entered and dropped their backpacks in a room on the right side of the hallway. "This could be promising."

Wendy Yost shut the door.

Jack fast-forwarded the video at the perfect speed so as not to miss anyone entering the room with the backpacks.

They watched.

They waited.

Tension coiled in Zoe's shoulders.

"Wait," Jack said, slowing the video to normal speed. A blonde woman, about Shannon's height and build, hesitated at the door.

Zoe sat straight. "I can't tell if it's her."

"We'll get a better look once she leaves the office."

A few minutes passed. Zoe reminded herself to breathe.

When the woman finally exited, she had flipped her hood over her head and backed out.

"It's like she knows where the camera is," Jack said softly.

"I don't think it's her."

"Why do you say that?"

"Her hoodie."

"What about it?"

"It's black."

"And…?"

"Shannon does not wear black. Ever. Trust me, I've seen her closet. She's a bright pink, lime green, tangerine kind of girl. Can you back it up?"

They watched the video again, Zoe hoping to discern more evidence proving it wasn't Shan.

"Interesting," Jack said.

"What?"

"That patch on her sleeve." He pointed to the screen, froze the image and zoomed in. "It looks like a bald eagle."

"I've never seen her wear animals on her clothes."

Head lowered, the hood blocking her profile, the woman turned and disappeared down the hall.

"Are there any other cameras?" Zoe said.

"The back parking lot. But let's keep an eye on this camera to see if the woman returns and we can get a better look."

They focused on the screen, but the woman did not reappear. Wendy Yost opened the office to let the kids in and when Jeanie got her backpack, she held it close and peeked inside. With a satisfied nod, she shouldered her pack and left.

"Looks like she got the product," Jack said.

"I'm not convinced it was Shannon who delivered it."

"I can see how you wouldn't be."

"What about you? What do you think?"

"I think we should examine more video."

Someone knocked on the door. "It's Detective Perry," a muffled voice said.

Jack put out his hand for Zoe to remain seated and he went to open the door.

Perry stepped inside. "When you're done with breakfast, I'll take you to identify the man we have in custody," he said to Zoe, ignoring Jack.

"I can finish this on the way." Zoe stood and closed the foam box. "Thanks for breakfast, Jack. You'll be here when I get back?"

"I'm coming with."

"You sure? You can stay here and finish your breakfast."

"I'll follow you."

"Okay."

She sensed the detective's displeasure as she accompanied him to his car. She'd offered Jack a pass by giving him permission to stay back. The man had a life, and since she was in police custody, she would be safe. Jack surely had work commitments to deal with, if not a search-and-rescue mission to join. She glanced at the clear sky.

"The weather's cleared up, so they'll be able to search for Shannon again, right?" she asked Detective Perry.

"Unfortunately the weather can be sunny down here, and completely opposite a thousand feet up. SAR Command decides if it's safe to send out teams."

She and Perry got into his dark sedan and

pulled away. She noticed Jack's SUV following them in the side view mirror.

"Although we haven't identified her yet, the victim they recovered from the mountain had drugs in her system and on her person," Detective Perry said. "We suspect she got high, went for a hike and fell, sustaining life threatening injuries."

Zoe shook her head. "Tragic. But why did she have Shannon's number?"

He didn't respond, probably expecting Zoe to fill in the blanks. The most obvious answer? The victim had her number because Shan was her drug supplier. Zoe still wouldn't accept that possibility.

"How do you and Jack Monroe know each other?"

She turned to him. "He's the one who rescued me off Mt. Stevens."

"You didn't know him before that?"

"No, why?"

"It seems like... Never mind."

"What?"

"It seems like you're awfully dependent on him considering you barely know the guy."

I know enough, she wanted to say. She realized how ridiculous that would sound, especially to a man like Detective Perry.

"He's been a good friend in the short time we've known each other."

"If you say so."

"Hey, why the attitude?" she challenged.

"I'm trying to solve a case here, while keeping you safe, and figure out what your friend got herself into."

"Nothing criminal."

He sighed. "I don't know who took her, but now someone's after you, and whoever it is knows where you're going to be before you even get there. Only four people knew you were staying at the inn—me, you, Sergeant Peterson and Jack Monroe."

"Let me understand this. First you accuse my best friend of being a drug dealer, and now you're accusing Jack of being involved in the kidnapping?"

"Being suspicious comes with the job."

"What about gut instinct? Isn't that part of the job?"

"You don't wanna know what my instinct says about Jack Monroe."

"Why, because he comes off as rude and arrogant?"

"He *is* rude and arrogant."

She realized Detective Perry was unable to look past his own perception to see another side of things.

"I don't see him that way," she said.

"Well, you should know his arrogance got Angie Adams killed."

"Hold on a second, you're blaming Jack for—"

"He tried to save her using basic first aid skills

when he should have called for a chopper to evac her out of there."

"What about the other members of Jack's team? Couldn't any of them call for help?"

"He was the team leader."

"And he jumped into action to save a girl's life."

"You weren't there."

"But you were?" she snapped.

He clenched his jaw.

She'd pushed back too hard but still, she didn't like the man maligning Jack's character for trying to save a girl's life.

"Okay, let's try again," she said, putting on her counselor's hat. "Angie's death is tragic, especially considering her friends abandoned her."

Perry snapped his attention to Zoe.

"Yes, Jack told me. How about you clue me in about what else is going on here."

"I'm a cop. I'm supposed to protect people, especially my own family members," he paused. "She shouldn't have died."

"Agreed. And Jack did everything he could to save her."

"If Monroe had called for a helicopter, they would have gotten her to the hospital that much sooner, and my niece would be alive today."

His niece? Whoa. Zoe let that one digest for a minute. Okay, it was making sense: why he was so angry at Jack, why Perry wanted to protect Zoe, why he didn't trust Jack.

"Detective, I am so sorry," she said.

"Now you know why you can't trust Jack Monroe."

"I understand why *you* feel you can't trust him. That has nothing to do with my situation."

"Be smart, and distance yourself from the guy."

"I appreciate your concern."

"But mind my own business."

"I didn't say that. The more people I have on my team protecting me, the better. Make no mistake, Jack is and will continue to be a member of that team."

They spent the next fifteen minutes in silence, Zoe considering the detective's words and then saying a prayer for his healing and his guilt. She could feel it oozing off him when he confessed that as a cop, he was committed to protecting his family. It had to be horrible to lose his niece the way he had, especially given the circumstances Jack had shared about the girl being abandoned by her friends.

Detective Perry pulled into the police department's parking lot.

"Sometimes it helps to talk about things," Zoe offered. "With a professional."

"What?" Perry turned off the engine.

"Your grief."

"Talking about it isn't going to change anything. Let's go."

He quickly got out of the car and she felt saddened by the shield of pain encasing the detective's heart. He'd never heal from the loss unless he walked straight into the fire of grief and came out the other side.

Jack joined her and Detective Perry, who led them into the police station. As they walked through the main office, Zoe noticed it was empty. Of course, their personnel were on the street patrolling neighborhoods.

"Wait here," Detective Perry said, motioning Zoe and Jack into a tidy office. "I'll bring you back when the lineup is ready."

Zoe sat in a chair opposite the walnut desk, but Jack remained standing, looking out the window.

Zoe's gaze drifted to a few framed photos of what she assumed were the detective's family. She understood his anger at Jack. Perry had to be angry with someone, and it was an act of self-defense to be upset with someone else, rather than look too closely at one's own guilt. It wasn't the detective's fault any more than it was Jack's.

"We talked about Angie in the car," she said.

Jack snapped around to look at her. "Why?"

"It just came up."

"You shouldn't talk about it, especially with him."

"Why not?"

"You just shouldn't." Jack looked back out the window.

"I don't suppose you've talked about it with anyone else either, have you?"

He didn't answer.

"Jack—"

"Don't involve yourself in this, Zoe. It's none of your business."

Again, someone else might consider his response rude. Zoe simply felt his pain.

"I'm sorry," she said.

He turned again and studied her. "Why? It's not your fault."

"Jack, me saying I'm sorry is me holding space for you, like before."

"Why would you do that?"

"What, hold space?"

He nodded.

"Because I can imagine the kind of pain you felt when you couldn't save Angie, and I want to be here for you so you won't feel so alone."

He shook his head.

"Still not computing, huh?" she said.

"I don't know."

Which was better than no.

Sudden, loud pops made Zoe shriek and she dove under the desk.

TEN

It was an automatic response on Zoe's part, having trained for the possibility of an active shooter event at school. She'd hoped, she'd prayed she'd never have to use her training.

Jack reached down and took her hand. "Get up. We're leaving."

Just like that. Without an edge of fear or concern or anything resembling the panic that hummed in her body.

She mimicked his affect and did as ordered.

As he guided her into the hallway, a door opened behind them and Detective Perry stumbled down the hall. Blood stained his shirt.

Jack froze and positioned Zoe behind him.

"Get her out of here," Perry said.

"You're wounded," Jack said.

"Out!" Perry ordered.

Jack hesitated a second, as if he didn't want to leave the man behind, but then turned and led Zoe away.

Silence rang in her ears. The shooting had stopped.

Her panic hadn't.

They approached the exit and Jack put his hand up to signal they should wait.

He listened.

She wondered what he heard that she didn't, and what was going on in that mind of his.

He looked at Zoe and nodded. He guided them to his SUV, and the doors unlocked with a click.

"Get in the back," he said.

She climbed in beside Romeo and wrapped her arms around the dog for comfort.

Jack got behind the wheel and they pulled away. "Call 911."

"Wouldn't they already know?" Zoe asked.

"Please, call 911," he repeated.

Good. Fine. He obviously had his wits about him, whereas Zoe was about to unravel. Again. Considering she thought herself a strong woman, she was certainly falling apart a lot lately. Of course she was—someone had opened fire in a police station.

Zoe made the call and reported shots fired at the sheriff's office.

"At the Mt. Stevens sheriff's office?" the operator repeated. "And with whom and I speaking?"

"Zoe Pratt. I was there for a lineup and someone opened fire and we escaped."

"Who's we?"

"Me and—"

Jack reached back and touched her knee.

She froze.

"No," Jack said.

"Ma'am?" the operator prompted.

She trusted that Jack knew what he was doing.

"Please send help. Call other police departments, send whoever you can." Zoe ended the call. "Why didn't you want me to say I'm with you?"

"I don't want them tracking my car, not right away."

"The police?"

"The shooters might have access to the frequency. I want to make sure you're safe, then I need time to think."

"Where are we going?"

"I don't know yet, maybe back to Portland."

"No, Jack, I need to stay in the area."

"That's not sensible."

"And you need to stay in the area to join the next search."

"There are plenty of other volunteers."

"But I have faith in you. Please, let's not run away from this."

"I do not want to see you hurt."

"Back at ya."

He glanced into the rearview mirror.

"We'll protect each other," she said.

We'll protect each other.

Was she kidding? How could Zoe protect Jack?

Then again, she'd talked both the teenager and the neighbor with the rifle out of shooting Jack. She had also neutralized the home intruder with her handy pepper spray.

Who was protecting whom here?

She didn't want to disappear, yet Jack didn't know any other way to avoid harm.

He'd been good at disappearing growing up when he felt threatened by bullies. He'd hide behind cabinets at school, or dive into a bush to camouflage himself, afterward feeling like a supreme loser.

That must be how Zoe felt when he suggested they leave town.

This was different. Her life was at stake.

He shot a quick glance into the rearview. Her eyes were closed, and she'd interlaced her fingers. Was she praying again?

A few seconds later she opened her eyes and caught him looking at her. He refocused on the road.

"Does praying help?" he asked.

"Absolutely, and it gave me an idea."

"What?"

"The Mt. Stevens Resort. Curt, the manager, offered me a room. I'll tell him, under no uncertain terms, not to let anyone know I'm there."

"I'd rather take you to Bellingham or Seattle."

"One night, okay? Depending on what happened at the police station, we'll make our next move tomorrow morning."

Their next move? Jack didn't think they had any moves left to play at this point. Shots fired at a police station meant both a bold villain and a serious breach of security. Was Detective Perry even still alive? Jack didn't like the man, but he didn't wish him harm. "Do you have the resort manager's number?"

"Yes." She dug into her shoulder bag and pulled out a business card. "Shall I call him?"

"Yes, make the arrangements."

She made the call. "Hi, Mr. Underwood. This is Zoe Pratt, Shannon's friend… No, no word about Shannon. I could use a room at the resort after all, if you can still make that happen… Sure, no problem. I'm on hold," she said to Jack. "Oh, hi again. Actually the isolated, private option would be great. Had kind of a crazy day… Can't go into it."

"Tell him to register under my name," Jack said.

"Also, can you put it under the name Jack Monroe? The fewer people who know where I'm staying the better… Yes, a lot of questions. Right. I could use the peace and quiet… Okay, great. Thanks." She ended the call. "Well, that's all set. They've got a duplex available right now if I want to check in early."

"We have to address a few things before we head over there."

"Like what?"

"Your appearance."

"What's wrong with my appearance?"

"You look like you."

"Wait, what? Ooohhh, you want me to look

like someone else, not like Zoe Pratt, who's being stalked because her friend was kidnapped."

"That is correct."

Jack was amazed by the way she boiled down the past few days of nonstop threat and danger into one concise sentence.

"Are you thinking hair dye, wig, what? It's not like I can eat my Wheaties and grow five inches."

"You're being funny or sarcastic?"

"A little of both. Again, it's my defense mechanism because I'm nervous."

He glanced in the rearview, but she was playing with Romeo and he couldn't see her eyes. Although her voice and her tone had a lightness to them, her meaning was very clear: she was, in fact, afraid about her current situation. And yet she was determined to stay in the area.

"To be clear, you want to stay in Mt. Stevens because…?"

"To clear Shannon's name."

"You'll need to keep a low profile."

"I understand that."

"You may not like what you find out…" he hesitated "…about your friend."

"Do you know something I don't?"

"No, but it's been my experience that people can surprise you, and not always in a good way."

"I love Shannon. There's nothing she could have done that would tarnish that love. It's unconditional. Like God's love is unconditional."

"For people who believe in Him."

"For everyone, Jack. We are all God's children."

Unconditional love. Interesting.

An hour and seventeen minutes later they had purchased supplies and Jack waited outside a gas station bathroom for Zoe to exit with her updated look.

She'd decided not to permanently dye her hair, because she said she'd tried that once and it turned out lime green. Instead, she'd bought a temporary spray-on color that her high school kids used. She'd also found a pair of glasses at the drugstore, and he'd managed to find the boots he was looking for at the country co-op store with two-inch heels to adjust her height. That and the monochromatic outfit and matching jacket would throw someone off track at first glance.

The bathroom door opened and she stepped out.

Maybe to anyone else she'd look plain and unremarkable, not worthy of a second glance. But to Jack she deserved a second, third and fourth glance. Beneath the all-black ensemble, gray-tinted hair and thick-rimmed glasses stood the enchanting Zoe Pratt. And she was looking at him.

"Well?" she said.

"Looks good." He hit the key fob to open his truck.

"But not good, right? I mean, I look boring, that was the plan?"

"Correct. That was the plan."

"Well, I think we've achieved that goal."

He motioned her into the truck and shut the door. Zoe Pratt could never look boring.

Jack scanned the surrounding area, including the burger restaurant parking lot next door for anything out of the ordinary, anything to indicate they were being followed or had been found. Although he didn't want Zoe telling Dispatch she was with Jack, he knew it was only a matter of time before authorities pieced it together, especially considering they'd been inseparable for three days.

He climbed into the front seat.

"I don't look that bad, do I, Romeo?" she asked his dog.

As Jack was about to clarify he didn't think she looked bad, just the opposite, his phone rang. He recognized Detective Perry's number. He hit the speaker button.

"Detective."

"I assume you still have Zoe?"

"I do."

"That was good work, getting her out of there unharmed."

"Thank you."

"Are you confident you can keep her safe?"

"I am."

"You do that and I'll focus on the case. Let me know where you end up."

"Are you all right?"

"No, I'm not all right. Someone assaulted my deputy and tried to break the perp out."

"Tried?"

"The perp's dead and his coconspirator fled the scene. Be on the lookout for a white minivan. Washington plates."

"Detective Perry, were you shot?" Zoe asked.

"Yeah, not serious. I'm going to text you a picture of the perp to determine if he was the intruder from the other night. Let me know. And check in periodically."

"Yes, sir," Jack said.

"Graham, you can call me Graham."

"Okay, we'll get back to you on the photo."

"Be safe."

"Thanks." Jack ended the call and passed the phone to Zoe.

"That was cool."

"What?"

"He wants you to call him by his first name."

"I don't understand why."

"It means he respects you, probably because you wanted to help him back at the police station."

"But I didn't help him."

"He sensed you wanted to, but getting me out of there was more important."

Jack puzzled over her comment. It was a natural reaction for him to want to assist the detective, especially since he'd been injured, but Jack had been torn. He needed to protect Zoe more.

He was certainly relieved that the detective didn't demand Jack return with Zoe to the sheriff's office. Not that the perp's coconspirator would make a reappearance, but because it would be traumatic for Zoe to have to reenter the building where gunfire had sent her diving under a desk. It had been a smart move on her part.

Jack felt there had been a shift in the communication channels between him and the detective. A good thing. He would rather have Detective Perry as an ally than an enemy. Jack and Zoe had enough enemies at present, including the weather, which was preventing teams from going back up to search for Shannon.

"We got Detective Perry's text," Zoe said, looking at Jack's phone. "It's the guy who broke into Shannon's place and assaulted you."

"Text the detective and let him know."

She did, then passed the phone back to Jack in the front seat. "So, the man who came for me at the inn wasn't the man who kidnapped Shannon, which means that guy still has her? And how many people are involved in this thing?"

"There's no way to tell."

"That was a rhetorical question."

"It didn't require an answer?"

"Nope, and yours wasn't very comforting," she muttered.

"I'm sorry." He needed to keep his mouth shut, wait for a clear signal that she expected an answer. Only, he wasn't sure he knew the right one to give.

She placed her hand on his shoulder. "It's okay. You're trying to be helpful and I'm overly emotional. Not a good combination."

"I didn't mean to make you feel bad."

"I know." She leaned back and petted Romeo.

Jack wished she was still resting her hand on his shoulder. When she touched him, the world seemed to make a little more sense. He wanted to do the same for her.

"Would it help to talk about the case or talk about something else?" he said.

"Definitely talk about solutions, possibilities, ways to bring this to resolution. Huh, I kinda sounded like you. You're rubbing off on me, Jack Monroe. So, I was able to retrieve the journal from the inn last night when I collected my things. Let's start there."

He heard her digging in her shoulder bag, and considered her words: *He* was rubbing off on *her*? He hoped not. Yet he could use some of her intuition and good nature to soften his edges. He heard the sound of pages flipping.

"Oh, right here she wrote about Randy, her boyfriend, that he was acting weird."

"Define weird."

"Knowing Shannon, that could mean he was withdrawn, quiet. She is quite a lively person and enjoys being around people who are upbeat and energetic, as well. I practically fell off the mountain trying to keep up with her on the trail."

"You did fall off the mountain."

"Not because I was clumsy. That jerk shoved me off."

"Right."

"If it hadn't been so slippery, I could've gotten the advantage."

"The advantage?"

"Kicked his kneecaps or done something to throw him off so we could have escaped."

"I'm sure you could have."

"Wait, are you teasing me? I thought you didn't have a sense of humor."

He shrugged. Maybe she was rubbing off on him after all.

"Shan also wrote about a subordinate who was giving her trouble, said he was skeegy."

"That is not a word."

"Shan made it up when we were kids. It means he was creepy, made her feel uncomfortable. His name is Walter Grosch. Maybe we should talk to him while we're at the resort. That would be easy and under the radar since he's already there, right?"

"Maybe easy, but perhaps not a good move if he's involved in this."

"True."

"I can do a check and see what pops up."

"Sounds good. I'd feel better knowing we're doing something and I'm not sitting around wallowing."

"I would feel better, too." Actually he felt better because she felt better. "We'll start with Walter. Then what?"

"It would be nice to talk to her boyfriend, exboyfriend, whatever he is. Who knows if or when he'll return. But he's not high on the suspect list since he's not even in town."

"That doesn't necessarily mean he's not involved."

"You make good arguments, you know that?"

"Is that bad?"

"Not at all. It keeps me sharp."

"There's the resort." He nodded. "Three hundred and twenty-five rooms. Tourists ski in the winter and hike in the summer. I'll pull up to the lobby and check in."

He pulled up and parked on the far end of the parking lot. "I'll be right back."

"He's coming right back, Romeo," Zoe said, petting the dog. Jack would return, they'd check her into the duplex, and she'd be safe.

For the time being. What would happen when he was called out on a mission? He couldn't be here 24/7, and he wouldn't have to be if they made progress on figuring out who kidnapped Shannon and why.

She thought about what he'd said, about the possibility she may not like what she found regarding Shannon. Fine, she would brace herself for the worst, but she still didn't believe it.

"'I can do all things through Christ who strengthens me,'" she said softly. And she could. She could stand up to the anonymous threat hounding her, and she could accept whatever truths they'd uncover about Shan.

A sudden tapping on the window made her jump. Kelly stood outside, waving. Zoe opened the door.

"I recognized Jack's car and was hoping you were inside," Kelly said. "You're not going to believe what happened."

"What?"

"Move over." Kelly climbed into the back seat and shut the door. "This." She held out her cell phone for Zoe to read.

Zoe was looking at a text…from Shannon.

"Whoa, I don't believe it."

"I didn't either, but it's her, and she's okay. Read it."

Zoe read the text: Got away from goon. In trouble. Don't tell police.

"Don't tell police?" Zoe looked at Kelly. "Why not?"

Kelly shrugged. "Have no idea. Did she text you?"

Zoe checked her phone. Nothing. "No. What are you going to do?"

"Not tell police, that's for sure."

"Hang on, shouldn't they know so they can send more search teams out? Maybe they can triangulate the location where the text came from or something. Jack would know about that stuff."

"She's my best friend and she asked me not to tell police, so I won't. I'm so glad she's okay."

"I wish we knew where she was and what's going on."

Kelly's phone beeped with another message.

"Is it Shannon?"

"No, my boss. Gotta run." Kelly leaned forward to give Zoe a hug, then left.

Zoe watched as Kelly crossed the parking lot and passed Jack. Kelly nodded her greeting, but didn't stop to chat, so Zoe figured she didn't share the news about Shannon.

Should Zoe? Yes, she should definitely tell Jack, no question. She trusted him implicitly. But how much should she share?

"Everything. He needs to know it all." Even if Zoe wasn't pleased about the *in trouble* part of the text. She needed to practice what she preached, and that meant unconditional love no matter what kind of trouble Shannon had gotten herself into.

She sighed, anxious for him to return, and considered the text. It seemed odd that Shannon referred to the kidnapper as a "goon." That didn't seem like a word Shan would have used. Even more odd that she'd texted Kelly instead of Zoe.

Jack slid into the front seat. "He reserved half a duplex in the northeast corner."

"Kelly got a text from Shannon."

Jack turned and looked at Zoe.

"Shan's text said she escaped the guy, but she's in trouble and not to tell police about the text."

Jack blinked his warm blue eyes, but didn't say anything.

"I'm ready. I can handle it." And she could. She waited for Jack to tell her they needed to call the police. Immediately.

"What do you want to do?"

"You're asking me?"

"Yes."

"Let's get settled. Then I'll call Detective Perry."

"Okay." He put the car in gear. "She could be in trouble because she got all turned around up there and can't find her way back. Did she mention any landmarks?"

"I didn't even think of it that way. No, she didn't mention landmarks. I'll text Kelly and ask her to reach out and see if Shan will respond."

"Why did you assume the mention of trouble was nefarious in meaning?"

"Because she said not to tell police, plus Shan didn't text me, she texted Kelly."

"And…?"

"I mean, I was with her up there when she was taken. I was shoved off a mountainside and you'd think she'd wonder if I was okay, and she'd know how upset I'd be about what I'd witnessed and…" Her voice trailed off. "Wow, I sound like a self-centered jerk."

"It's normal to say things out of character when you're upset."

"In other words, I'm not usually a self-centered jerk?"

"That's rhetorical again?"

"I guess."

"Don't do that."

"What?"

"Be hard on yourself. I don't think many friends would have stuck around like you have, considering the danger you're in."

"Yeah, and I am so done with being a target. I want Shannon back and safe."

They pulled up to a duplex and he turned to her. "Then let's focus on finding answers."

Zoe and Jack spent the afternoon going through Shannon's journal and making up a chart to guide their investigation. He realized he'd never been this comfortable working with a partner. He'd been a one-man team, ever since childhood.

Yet Zoe and Jack bounced ideas off each other, which stimulated new ideas, new avenues to explore. She had shared the information from Shannon's text with Detective Perry hours ago. Jack had hoped that would move the investigation forward, but it was nearly dinnertime and they hadn't heard back from the detective.

He noticed her constantly checking her phone, probably hoping for a text from Shannon. It seemed like the absence of such a text further wounded Zoe each time she looked at her phone.

Jack wanted to distract her but wasn't sure how.

Her phone vibrated and her eyes lit with hope, then quickly dimmed.

"It's Curt. Walter Grosch has arrived for his shift." Zoe looked at Jack. "We should question him."

"Not here. Ask Curt to suggest an alternate location on the property."

She responded. "Need a place to meet. Not our duplex," she said as she texted. She sat down at the kitchen table. Her anxiety was palpable.

"You could stay here and let me talk to him alone," Jack suggested, although truth be told, he didn't want to leave her.

"No, I need to do this." Her phone pinged with a text. "He's sending Walter to meet us at the storage facility on the north end of the property."

"Okay, let's go." They got their coats on and Romeo thought it was time to work. "Romeo, stay."

The dog lay down, but didn't look happy.

Jack asked her to wait for him to exit first, so he could be sure to scan the surrounding area. No one should know where they were, but he didn't want to take any chances. They shouldn't have found Zoe at the inn either, or at the police station, although that incident seemed to be related to breaking out the suspect, not kidnapping Zoe.

They headed north in his SUV.

"I hope Walter is helpful," Zoe said.

"Aren't you worried that he's skeegy?"

"Very funny."

"I wasn't making a joke."

"Oh, sorry. No, I'm not worried because you're with me."

Jack's chest swelled with pride. As he drove to the storage facility, he wondered if he should have called Detective Perry. Too late now. Besides, Walter didn't have a record or even a speeding ticket for that matter. He was a retired schoolteacher. Harmless.

The facility was a tall, gray building with a metal roof and large barn-type doors. Spotlights illuminated the property. One of the barn doors was open about three feet.

"Curt told him to wait inside for us," Zoe said.

When Jack parked, she reached for the door. "Are you sure you don't want to stay in the car?" Jack said.

"No, absolutely not."

He studied her face, wondering if she genuinely meant no, or if she was putting up a brave front. After all, the guy was *skeegy*.

"That's really no, Jack," she said. "I want to go with you."

He nodded, and they exited the SUV. He motioned for her to stay behind him. Apparently the gunfire from this morning had left its mark on Jack's psyche, as well.

He slowly entered the storage facility. Floor-to-ceiling shelves ran down the center of the building and also bordered the outside walls.

He felt Zoe take his hand. Warmth crept up his arm and he gave her hand a squeeze, letting her know everything was going to be okay, although he didn't know that for certain. He didn't have instincts like other people, couldn't always tell when something was amiss, as evidenced by Jeanie's attack with a gun.

"Walter?" Zoe called out. "Walter Grosch?"

Silence answered them. Then a clicking sound echoed from the other end of the building. Jack put his finger to his lips and led her down an aisle. He wasn't letting her go now, not if his life depended on it.

Then Jack reconsidered his direction. The sound could be designed to lure them into a position of vulnerability.

He turned to head back to the SUV, he wasn't sure why.

"You're not going to get me!" a man shouted.

ELEVEN

Jack shoved Zoe aside and ducked, but the two-by-four connected with Jack's shoulder.

"No!" Zoe shouted.

"Get out of here!" Jack ordered.

The board came down a second time across Jack's back. At least it wasn't his head. Jack scrambled to get away from the attacker.

"I'm not taking the fall for you!" the guy shouted. He sounded crazed, out of his mind.

As Jack braced himself for another blow, he saw Zoe pull something out of her bag.

"Get away from him!" she ordered.

"Aaahhh!" the man cried out.

She'd nailed him with the pepper spray.

Jack got to his feet and stood beside Zoe, who pointed the spray at the guy's face. The man, mid-sixties with graying hair, stumbled backward. But he still clung to the piece of wood.

"My eyes!" he shouted. "You blinded me!"

"It's pepper spray. It's temporary," Zoe said. "Why did you attack us?"

"He warned me you were coming. I'm not going to jail for you. You can't prove I'm involved." He waved the board in front of him, unable to see his targets, but determined to keep Zoe and Jack away.

"Calm down," Jack said.

"I don't have the drugs!" He turned to run.

"No, wait!" Zoe said, following him.

"Zoe," Jack grabbed her arm to put distance between them and the crazed man. He disappeared around the corner.

A shriek and a grunt echoed through the facility. Jack and Zoe rushed to the end of the aisle.

Kelly stood over the man's still body on the floor. Blood seeped from a head wound. Kelly dropped her weapon, a metal pipe. "Walter," she said. "What have I done?"

So, this was Walter.

"Kelly, call 911," Zoe ordered.

Zoe went to Walter's side, whipped off her scarf and held it against the wound on his head. It seemed like he tried opening his eyes, but they were swollen from the pepper spray.

"Walter, it's okay," Zoe said. "We're calling the paramedics."

"No police. They'll arrest me."

"Why would they arrest you?" she said.

"My back," he said.

"You hurt your back just now?"

"No, that's why I needed the drugs. Got them from her…so I could work."

Zoe wasn't sure if she wanted to ask the next question. "Shannon sold you drugs?"

Walter nodded and closed his eyes.

"Walter?" Zoe placed her ear to his chest. A strong heartbeat.

"He's still alive." She looked at Jack, who was making the 911 call.

Kelly crumbled to her knees beside Zoe, hugging herself. "I didn't know what else to do. I thought he was going to hurt you and I couldn't let him hurt Shannon's best friend."

"Jack, can you take over here?" Zoe said.

As Jack knelt, she noticed him wince slightly.

"How's your back?" she said.

"Take care of Kelly."

He pressed the scarf against Walter's head wound and Zoe turned to Kelly. "It's okay, Walter's going to be okay."

"I didn't…kill him, did I?"

"No, you didn't kill him."

Kelly glanced at Zoe with fear in her eyes. "Are they going to arrest me?"

"No, you didn't do anything wrong."

Zoe spent the next few minutes consoling Kelly as they waited for police to arrive. The young woman was coming apart, traumatized by the violent action she'd taken to defend Zoe and Jack.

I couldn't let him hurt Shannon's best friend.

Speaking of best friends, Zoe wondered if she really knew Shan at all.

A drug dealer? Walter was the second person to claim as much. Even if they were able to prove it wasn't Shan who put the drugs in Jeanie's backpack at the community center, what explanation could there be about Walter's story?

Zoe's phone rang with a call from Curt, the resort manager. "I need to take this. Are you okay?" she asked Kelly.

"Yes," Kelly said, still staring at Walter.

Zoe stood and answered. "Hi, Curt."

"I saw an ambulance speeding by the main building. Is everyone okay?"

"Walter attacked us." She glanced at his still body.

Kelly leaned close to him. "I'm sorry, Walter. I'm so sorry."

"Attacked you? Why would he—"

"I think he's on drugs." She'd sensed as much from his crazed behavior and dilated pupils. "I'll call you back after police take our statements."

"Police?"

"This might be tied to their investigation into Shannon's disappearance. I've gotta go."

Jack opened the barn doors wide and waved emergency crews into the storage facility.

Detective Perry stormed up to Jack. "You were supposed to keep her safe."

"He did," Zoe said. "I'm fine. Walter isn't."

"Who assaulted him?"

"I got him with pepper spray, then Kelly hit him with a pipe," Zoe said. "She was defending me and Jack. Walter was acting crazed and violent. Kept saying he didn't want to go to jail."

Two paramedics took Walter's vitals. "Anyone

know if he's on anything?" the younger of the two asked.

"I suspect so, but don't know what," Zoe offered.

After a few minutes they shifted Walter onto a stretcher. Kelly didn't move from her position on her knees. It was as if she still thought Walter was on the ground in front of her.

"Come on," Zoe said, encouraging her to stand.

Kelly stood, wearing a dazed look on her face.

"Why were you two out here anyway?" Perry said.

Sergeant Peterson entered the storage facility and joined them.

"Shannon mentioned Walter in her journal," Zoe explained. "We wanted to meet him and ask some questions."

"Why, because you think you can do my job better than I can?" Detective Perry directed his question at Jack.

"It was my idea," Zoe said. "And I think you're doing a fine job, but we were already here, and I thought it wouldn't hurt to get a little more information for you, for the case."

Detective Perry slowly turned his gaze to Zoe. "And what did you find out?"

Her heartbeat pounded into her eardrums as she mustered the courage to admit everything they'd learned. She wouldn't look at Jack because she didn't want the detective to think he had undue influence over her.

"Walter claimed that Shannon was selling him drugs."

"We're losing him!" a paramedic shouted as they hesitated in the doorway.

Zoe put her arm around a whimpering Kelly.

"I didn't hit him that hard," Kelly said, turning into Zoe's shoulder to look away from the scene. Zoe felt Jack's arm slide around her. The three of them waited, listening to the sounds of paramedics trying to keep Walter alive.

"Clear!" a man shouted.

Zoe jerked at the sound of paddles shocking a heart back to life.

Long, grueling minutes stretched by as Zoe tried to block out the sound of the paramedics, trying to revive Walter.

"I didn't hit him that hard," Kelly repeated.

"Shhh," Zoe said, patting her back.

"Come on," Jack said, leading Zoe and Kelly to the other side of the storage facility.

Detective Perry and Sergeant Peterson didn't follow, which was good since their presence upset Kelly. She probably thought they'd arrest her for murder if Walter didn't make it.

But why? Why wouldn't he make it? It was true, Kelly didn't hit him that hard, and the pepper spray wouldn't cause cardiac arrest.

"Got a heartbeat. Let's go!"

Zoe sighed and closed her eyes. *Thank you, God.*
She felt Jack squeeze her shoulder and she
looked at him. He offered what she interpreted as
a subtle and comforting smile as if to say *it's okay*.

But it wasn't okay. It was looking more and
more like Shannon was involved in the drug business.

And she was still missing.

Nothing was okay.

Jack led the women back to the opposite side of
the storage facility to finish their interview with
Detective Perry.

"Jack, you okay?" Sergeant Peterson said.

It was only then that Jack felt the warm trickle
of blood seeping down the side of his head. "I'm
fine," he said.

Curt entered the facility, but Detective Perry
put out his hand. "This is a crime scene. Please
stay out."

Jack agreed. The fewer people in here, the
better. More people would confuse the situation,
maybe even upset the women further.

He sensed how distraught Zoe was by the tension in her shoulders. The more they dug into her
friend's life, the more evidence they uncovered
that Shannon was a drug dealer. Jack wished he
could give Zoe comfort, but he knew he'd fall
short in that department. Wasn't that what Mari
had said when she broke off their relationship?

That Jack was missing the skills necessary to ful-fill a woman in the emotions department?

Now why was he going there, he wondered. Head injury, no doubt.

"Am I going to jail?" Kelly asked the detective.

"I'm not arresting you for trying to protect Jack and Zoe," Detective Perry said. "Jack, you're next." He motioned Jack to follow him, away from the women.

Jack didn't like the idea of being even a few feet away from Zoe, but at least he could still see her. He gave Perry an official statement, pretty much repeating what Zoe had said.

"Is there anything else? Anything Zoe didn't mention?"

"I'm not sure I understand your meaning."

He narrowed his eyes. "You're a smart guy, smarter than most. Maybe you picked up on some-thing she didn't because she was blinded by loy-alty to her friend."

Jack thought about that for a moment. "Well, the assault seemed personal."

"Personal how?"

"Walter seemed like he had targeted me specifi-cally, but I never met the man until today. I can't explain it." And he couldn't because he wasn't a people or behavior expert.

"What gave you that idea, that it was personal?"

"Something he said, that he was warned about us, that I was coming to get him."

"He knew you were coming? Maybe you need to relocate."

"No, he meant here, at the storage facility. He said, 'I'm not going to jail for you. You can't prove I'm involved.'"

"Involved?"

"Drugs? As Zoe told you, Walter admitted he bought drugs from Shannon."

Detective Perry glanced at Zoe, who was still consoling Kelly. "How's Zoe taking it? The confirmation that her friend is a drug dealer?"

"I don't know."

Detective Perry frowned at Jack. "You need to be up front with me, that was the agreement from the beginning—share information about Zoe to help the investigation."

"I'm not keeping anything from you."

"I wish I could believe that."

"I do not lie to the authorities."

"No, but you could be holding back."

"Could be, but I'm not. I haven't had a chance to speak with Zoe alone to find out how she's processing all this. How much longer will we be detained?"

"Almost done."

"What about the text from Shannon to Kelly?" Jack asked.

"I spoke with Kelly earlier. That was the only one she received. We don't have the tools to track the phone to an exact location, but they're trying to triangulate a general area."

"I could do it."

Perry eyed him.

"If I can't pinpoint the exact location, then it can't be done."

"Yeah, okay, hotshot."

Jack noted the sarcasm. "It's my business. It's what I'm good at."

"I'll think about it."

"Were you able to trace the car that left the scene of the police department shooting?"

Jack must have said the wrong thing because the detective's countenance seemed to harden even more. "The minivan had been reported stolen by Curt Underwood."

"From the resort?"

"No, he'd parked it at the Village Supermarket, and when he came out, it was gone. We found it three miles outside of town. Working on prints now. In the meantime, why don't you head back to your lodging and keep a low profile? I'll post a deputy in an unmarked car on the property. Don't leave the premises for any reason, you got me?"

"I understand the wisdom of your concern, but I cannot dictate what Zoe does or does not do."

"Well, you'd better learn to dictate, Jack. I don't want to lose her, too, because you failed."

The detective, whom Jack would obviously no longer call by his first name, turned abruptly and walked away. Jack stood there, feeling like...like what? He felt like he'd been kicked in the stomach with a steel-tipped boot. Twice.

These past few days his focus had been to keep Zoe safe, yet the detective was calling Jack a failure for not being able to control her decisions, her actions.

No, the detective was doing much worse: he was blaming Jack, to his face, for Angie Adams's death.

Jack knew some people questioned his actions up on the mountain; he even questioned himself from time to time, when his mind drifted, when he wasn't absorbed in one project or another. But his team said he'd made the right call, done his best to administer emergency aid. They'd said it wasn't his fault that the chopper didn't make it in time because it was on another assignment.

"Did you really just say that to him?"

Jack glanced up. Zoe was blocking Detective Perry.

"Excuse me?" Perry said.

"That snarky remark about Jack losing me, too? He wasn't the sole person responsible for Angie's death, Detective, and to suggest as much is utterly cruel. You need to get right with yourself about what happened to your niece before you start casting blame on others."

Jack went to intervene, but Zoe put out her

hand, as if she wouldn't allow him to speak on his own behalf.

With fire in her eyes, she glared at the detective. "This is bullying behavior and it's unacceptable. They say bullies are victims, that they've been bullied themselves. I think you've been beating yourself up over your loss, and now you've aimed that frustration and self-loathing at Jack. It needs to stop because it's only causing more friction and confusion when we're trying to find my friend and apparently shut down a drug ring. Isn't that our goal?"

"It is," Perry said.

"Then deal with your grief and leave us out of your misery."

Silence blanketed the storage facility. Sergeant Peterson glanced at his phone and frowned. Another deputy, who was collecting evidence, looked away.

Zoe held the detective's gaze, not backing down. "Are we done?"

"For now."

She glanced at Jack. "Take me back?"

"Of course," Jack said.

Then she turned to Kelly, who was still staring blindly at the spot where Walter had landed after she'd hit him. Her boss, Curt, was patting her shoulder.

"Kelly, do you want to come with us?" Zoe asked.

"I'm going to drop her at her parents' house," Curt said.

"Good, she shouldn't be alone." Zoe gave Kelly a hug. "Thank you for defending us. It will all be okay."

Back at the duplex Zoe's prayers had changed. Well, not changed completely, but they had been amended. Instead of praying solely for Shannon's safe return, Zoe also started praying for strength to deal with the potential reality of her friend being a drug dealer.

"No, I simply won't believe it," she whispered as she gazed out the window of the suite. She stood behind the curtain so no one outside could see her standing there. Along with sunset came more snow, which meant no search teams would be sent into the mountains.

That's when Zoe realized it didn't matter if Shan had gotten involved in something shady. She was still loved, unconditionally, both by Zoe and God.

"Thank you," Jack said.

Zoe glanced at him, but he didn't look up from his laptop. "For what?"

"What you said to Detective Perry."

"You're welcome, although I'm a bit embarrassed about that."

That made him look at her. "Why?"

"I kind of lost it. You don't think I was too harsh?"

"Sometimes harsh is necessary."

"I know, but I do feel sorry for the man. Yet I can't stand watching someone be abused because the abuser hasn't dealt with his own pain." She went to Jack and glanced over his shoulder. "Any luck finding Shan's phone?"

"Not yet." He tapped away at his keyboard, as if not wanting to give up, although she sensed it was a lost cause. Romeo slept contentedly by Jack's feet.

"I know you're doing your best." She placed her hand on his shoulder.

His fingers stopped.

She snatched her hand away. "Sorry, I shouldn't touch you while you're concentrating."

"No, it's okay," he said. He continued to type in code of some kind. "It makes no sense."

"What?" She went to the kitchenette and turned on the stove to warm water.

"Are you making tea?" Jack said.

"Yes, you want some?"

"Please."

"What makes no sense?"

"My program, designed to track a GPS signal, keeps giving me a bounce back."

"Meaning?"

"It's giving me Kelly's phone location, instead

of Shannon's. I'm not sure how they're doing that, rerouting the location to the receiving phone."

"So we're dealing with someone who's tech savvy?"

"Yeah, but more tech savvy than me?" he said.

"Ego much?" She winked.

He half frowned.

"Teasing again," she said. "You sounded so surprised, maybe even horrified that someone could be better at this tech stuff than you. It's kinda cute."

His frown deepened at that comment.

"Don't listen to me," she said. "I'm worn out, hungry, confused, maybe a little sad."

"Tea will help."

She felt herself smile slightly at his comment. Jack thought he could assuage her emotional turmoil with the mention of tea. She appreciated his intention.

"And food," he said. "I'll call the restaurant and place an order." He stood and went to the bureau where he pulled out a leather-bound resort directory that included a restaurant menu. "You want a burger, sandwich, fish dinner…?" He glanced up. "What sounds good?"

For half a second, she wasn't a grieving friend, worried about Shannon, sucked into a maelstrom of danger. Zoe was a woman being asked to make a decision about dinner.

Jack studied her, then looked back at the menu.

"Or if that doesn't sound good, they serve breakfast all day, even at night."

"Thank you."

He glanced up again. "For what?"

"For making me feel a little normal during all this craziness."

"I'm not sure how I did that."

"Just say 'you're welcome.'"

"You're welcome?" And he shared a curious smile.

"I'll take a turkey sandwich on wheat."

"Okay. I'll place our orders."

"And fries."

"With ranch dressing?"

"Ooohhh, I never through of dipping fries in ranch. Sure, I'll try that."

As Jack called in their order, Zoe found tea bags in a cupboard. The food would do her good. No doubt the drop in her blood sugar was contributing to her morose mood.

Her phone pinged with a text. Kelly was texting for an update. Zoe felt so frustrated. How could she respond that Shannon was a criminal?

She wouldn't, because Zoe wasn't 100 percent convinced of that fact herself. All indications pointed to Shannon's involvement, but Zoe clung to hope that it was a mix-up.

"Okay, thanks." Jack hung up the phone and went to join her in the kitchenette. "It will be here in thirty to forty minutes."

"I'm not satisfied," Zoe said.

"Well, it is the dinner hour so they're pretty busy."

"I'm talking about Shannon. I mean, a nice, Christian woman doesn't suddenly become a drug dealer." She started pacing, thoughts spinning in her brain. Was she onto something here? Or was this the last vestiges of denial?

The kettle whistled, and she went to pour hot water over the tea bags. "What's her motivation? She didn't live extravagantly, and was driving a fifteen-year-old Honda."

"Those cars do last a long time."

"She dressed humbly, didn't take vacations, didn't own expensive jewelry, and the house she rented was modest at best. Where is all the money that she would have made from dealing drugs?"

"I don't have an answer."

"Because there's no evidence of her receiving large sums of money. Someone doesn't become a drug dealer, make a ton of money and not spend it. Can you break into her financial records?"

"Break in?"

"Sorry, access her financial information? Credit cards, stuff like that?"

"I shouldn't."

"Please?"

He glanced down. She touched his arm and he looked at her, his blue eyes brighter than normal.

"I need to help my friend, Jack."

With a nod, he went back to his laptop.

Half an hour later, Jack said he was close to accessing Shan's accounts.

Zoe paced, feeling both hopeful and guilty about what they were doing. If it would somehow support Shan's innocence, it was worth the risk.

"Okay, I'm in," he said.

She rushed across the room and stood beside him.

They scanned her deposits, withdrawals and online payments, checking everything they could think of to find evidence of her friend's extreme spending behavior.

"What do you think?" she said.

"I don't see anything unusual here. We've gone back six months, yet there are no cash deposits."

"That's good, right?"

"Hmm."

"Hmm, what?"

He tapped away, opening screens and closing others. She couldn't make sense of what he was doing.

"It looks like someone else may have accessed her accounts," he said.

There was a knock at the door.

"Dinner," Jack said, still focused on his laptop screen.

"I'll get it." Zoe started for the door.

"No, Zoe—"

The door flew open and three men burst into the suite.

TWELVE

Romeo barked protectively but kept his distance.

"Hands where I can see them, and control that dog," one of the intruders ordered. He was a tall, skinny man wearing dark pants and jacket.

"Romeo, right here," Jack said.

The dog sat beside him, and Jack raised his hands.

"Identify yourselves," Jack said, not that he had any leverage in this situation.

"DEA. Hands behind your head. Now."

Jack did as they ordered, glancing at Zoe who seemed more angry than upset. Good. He hated seeing her upset. "What's this about?" he asked.

One of the other agents, short and stocky, wearing a leather jacket and permanent scowl, zip-tied Jack's wrists and led him to the sofa. Romeo followed and jumped up beside Jack. A low growl rumbled from his throat.

"Romeo, quiet," Jack said.

The stocky agent motioned for Zoe to sit beside Jack. She did and crossed her arms over her chest, denying them the access to restrain her. They most likely didn't force the issue because they didn't consider her a physical threat.

Zoe and Jack were so close that their thighs touched. He hoped the contact would calm her because he didn't want her spouting off at the agents and escalating the situation.

"I'm Agent Trotter," the tall, skinny agent said. "Is that your laptop?"

"Yes, sir," Jack answered.

Agent Trotter motioned for the third agent, the youngest of the group with red hair, to sit at the table. He opened the laptop and tapped on the keyboard. He hesitated and looked at Jack. "Password?"

"Romeo1215_&#." A password he'd quickly change once he got his laptop back.

Agent Trotter motioned for the stocky agent to stand watch by the door, then swung a chair backward, straddled it and studied Zoe and Jack.

"How are you involved with Shannon Banks?" Agent Trotter said.

"Involved?" Jack said.

"In her drug operation."

"She's not involved with drugs," Zoe snapped.

The room fell quiet. Agent Trotter eyed her. "And you are?"

"I'm Shannon's best friend, Zoe. I was with her when she was taken."

Trotter turned to Jack, expectant.

"I'm Jack Monroe with Search and Rescue. I found Zoe last Friday after she fell off the mountain—"

"Was pushed," Zoe interrupted.

"—and was injured," Jack finished.

"You were the one who accessed Miss Banks's personal accounts?"

"I am," Jack said.

"Then you're under arrest."

"He was doing me a favor," Zoe said. "I'm trying to prove Shannon's not a drug-dealing criminal."

"How about it, Red?" Agent Trotter said to the agent working intently on Jack's laptop.

"They didn't move anything around," the agent said. "Just went exploring."

"Ask Detective Perry," Zoe said. "He can tell you we're not involved. I'm trying to help my friend and in the meantime, I've become a target."

"Maybe because you keep doing things like breaking into bank accounts."

"If she's a drug dealer, where's the money?" Zoe said.

"Zoe," Jack said, trying to temper her.

"We couldn't find it," Zoe said. "Could you? No, because she's not involved. You've got the wrong suspect, and she's probably up in the mountains dying a slow, miserable death while we're all down here more focused on a phantom drug ring than saving her life."

Agent Trotter tapped his fingers on the chair. Jack feared they were both going to be arrested.

No, he couldn't let that happen. "It was my idea to access Shannon Banks's accounts. Arrest me." He turned to Zoe. "Take care of Romeo."

"Jack, no," she said in a soft voice, as if she were in pain.

He was trying to protect her, yet only managed to upset her further.

"Where's your cell phone?" Agent Trotter asked Zoe.

"In my bag," she said. "Side pocket."

The stocky agent retrieved her cell phone.

"Is Detective Perry's number in here?" Trotter said.

"Yes," Zoe said.

Trotter motioned for the stocky agent to give her the phone. "Call him. Tell him to come over."

As she made the call, Jack puzzled over why the agent didn't call Detective Perry himself.

It didn't completely surprise Jack that their paths had crossed with the Drug Enforcement Agency. Since this mystery seemed rooted in a drug distribution business, it was only a matter of time before they appeared. Jack sensed they were not working hand in hand with local law enforcement or else the DEA agents would have known whose room they were breaking into tonight.

"Someone's coming," the stocky agent said, peering through the curtains.

"Room service," Jack offered. "Zoe hasn't eaten since eleven this morning." He didn't care if they kept him restrained, but he wanted her to be comfortable.

"What do you want me to do?" asked the agent by the window.

Trotter nodded at Zoe. "Don't let him in. Take the food and close the door."

She stood and went to retrieve her purse.

"What are you doing?" Trotter asked.

"I need to tip him." She grabbed cash out of her wallet, went to the door and waited, seemingly irritated. The stocky agent flanked the other side of the door.

Jack presumed that the DEA didn't want it to be common knowledge they were close to nailing the drug ring, for fear the players might disappear. By tracking Jack's activity today, they probably thought they had found one of the key suspects in this scheme.

The resort employee knocked, and Zoe opened the door. "Hi, thanks."

"I can set it up for you in the—"

"No, I'm good. I'll take the tray."

A moment later she kicked the door shut and carried a tray over to the kitchen table.

"Can I sit at the table or is being hungry against the law?" she said.

Jack wondered why she thought sarcasm was a good idea in this situation. Then again, she relied on sarcasm when she was anxious.

"You've got quite an attitude for someone who's about to be arrested," Trotter said.

"For what? For loving my friend so much I want to prove her innocence?"

She and the agent stared at each other, and Zoe didn't back down. Jack knew she was strong but didn't know how strong she was until this very moment. She had pushed through the fear of the past few days and had come out the other side a tenacious woman.

"Go ahead and eat," Trotter said.

"Jack needs to eat, too."

"Don't push it."

"Look, I'm a social worker for teens, and Jack's an IT entrepreneur. We're out of our league here, I know that, but we're trying to do the right thing for an innocent woman who was taken against her will."

"Or she disappeared of her free will."

"You weren't there," Zoe said, her voice low. "You didn't see how the man brutalized her… and me."

"You could be covering for her."

"Do a background check on me, go on. And do one on Jack. He's got nothing to hide either."

An interesting assumption on her part, although she was right, Jack had a squeaky-clean background.

Trotter studied her, still assessing.

"We're trying to help you," she said.

"By getting involved in police business?"

"By proving she's not your suspect so you can focus on finding the real criminal."

Agent Trotter narrowed his eyes.

"Are you going to let Jack eat dinner with me?" Zoe asked.

Trotter motioned with his hand.

Jack stood, waiting for someone to remove the cuffs.

"Zip ties stay on," Trotter said.

His ego swelled at the thought that these three men thought Jack could physically overtake them.

"Come on," Zoe said. "I'll feed you."

He hesitated, not wanting to be embarrassed by being spoon-fed.

"Jack, the food will get cold."

She motioned the tech agent to move aside and she sat down, lifting the cover off one of the plates. She pulled out a chair and Jack joined her at the table.

"Haven't you been working with the local police on this case?" she asked Agent Trotter.

"No."

"Why not?" She dipped a French fry in ranch dressing.

"Because they suspect someone in the sheriff's office is involved," Jack guessed.

Trotter sat across the table from him. "Why would you say that?"

"It's the most logical assumption as to why you

are keeping your investigation hidden from local authorities."

Zoe held a ranch-dipped fry to Jack's mouth and he ate it, surprised that he wasn't embarrassed at being fed like a child.

"My turn for questions," Trotter said.

"Don't you have to read us our rights first?" Jack said.

"Only if he's going to arrest us, which he hasn't," Zoe said.

"Yet," Trotter said.

Zoe shook her head, then dipped another fry in ranch.

"What's with the shaking of the head?" Trotter said.

"I'm so over all this bullying. Bullying and threats. Which is what I thought I was taking a break from back at work."

"I'm not bullying," Trotter said.

"You were threatening. Same thing. Whatever, ask your questions." She bit into her fry and her expression softened as she looked at Jack. "This is good."

Jack took pride in the fact she liked his food suggestion.

"What makes you think Shannon Banks is innocent?" Agent Trotter said.

"I've known her since we were kids. She's a good person. There's no evidence of a money trail or large purchases, the kinds of things someone who was making illegal money would buy. I'm assuming you already knew that, so what makes her your number one suspect?"

When Trotter didn't answer, Zoe continued, "I've got a clean record. Jack's got a clean record. We're obviously not involved, but like I said before, we'd like to scratch Shannon off your suspect list."

"I doubt that will happen."

"Why's that?"

"Because one of our agents was with her when she smuggled drugs across the border from Canada."

Zoe's hand, holding a French fry, froze and her face drained of color. She slowly put the fry back on the pile. She looked like she'd lost her best friend which, in a sense, she had.

Jack fisted his hands, wanting the zip ties gone. He wanted to wrap his arms around her and hold her close.

"I don't believe you," she said.

"Excuse me?" Agent Trotter said, indignant.

"Give her a minute," Jack said. "She's processing."

"You're saying you're her best friend, yet you had no idea?" Trotter said.

Zoe shook her head. Jack wondered if she was unable to speak because she was angry or devastated, or a little of both.

"Did the agent see the drugs?" Zoe said.

"Eventually, when they returned to the resort."

"Oh." Zoe sat back and crossed her arms over her chest. "Who was this agent? You trust him?"

"Yes. Randy Green is one of our top guys."

"Randy? Her boyfriend?"

"That was his undercover assignment—to get close to Shannon Banks. And now he's gone, too."

"Gone?"

"Missing. He hasn't checked in for days. We suspect her people took him out."

"You're making it sound like Shannon was a drug lord with a team of hired killers on her payroll."

"This new drug is an incredibly profitable hybrid with intense effects. It's offered in pill form, liquid, or even gummy candy for kids."

"Shannon would never—"

"Maybe she had good intentions, who knows. A little can manage pain, but users can't stop with a little. After a few months they start to need more and more until they can't responsibly dose themselves, leading to irrational behavior and hallucinations. A teenager in Tacoma took too much and jumped off a bridge. We're trying to prevent that from happening again."

"That's tragic, but Shan is not involved. Wait, back up. She loved Randy, and he was…using her?"

"We're trying to keep drugs out of the hands of children."

"Shannon worked as a volunteer *with* children. You think she wants to get them hooked? That makes no sense."

"The only thing that *does* make sense is that she's involved in a drug ring, she knew we were onto her and she faked her own kidnapping and disappearance."

"You weren't there. You didn't see what happened. The kidnapper tried to kill me. Shannon would never let that happen."

"Or, she lost control of the situation."

"Enough. I don't want to hear any more. My friend is still missing."

"So is my agent, and if anything happens to him, we'll be adding kidnapping and murder to the charges against Shannon Banks."

"Someone's here," the third agent said from the window. "Looks like a cop."

"Detective Perry," Trotter said.

The situation was going from bad to worse, Jack thought. He sensed Zoe's emotions were strung tighter than a tennis racket. Adding Perry and his chip-on-the-shoulder attitude to the equation would only exacerbate things.

"Are you going to arrest me?" Jack said.

Zoe glared at Agent Trotter, her jaw clenched.

"Let's see what Detective Perry says."

Zoe shared a look with Jack. Perry was not their champion, which meant Jack might be spending the night in jail.

Perry knocked on the door.

Romeo sat up, ready to charge.

"Romeo, stop," Jack said.

The dog flopped down with a harrumph.

The agent opened the door to Detective Perry.

"Who are you?" Perry said, then stepped into the room. He frowned at the sight of Zoe and Jack sitting at the table with Agent Trotter, Jack's hands secured behind him. "What's going on here?"

Agent Trotter stood and flashed his badge. "Agent Trotter, DEA. Have a seat."

"I'll stand, thanks. Let me guess, you've been investigating Shannon Banks for months, but didn't bother to inform my department."

"That is correct."

"Why?"

"We suspect someone in local law enforcement might be involved."

"Great, that's just great. You keep me in the dark, then accuse someone on my team of being dirty. What about them? Why are you harassing Jack and Zoe?"

"Our tech agent caught someone accessing Shannon Banks's accounts and we followed the IP address here. Jack Monroe accessed the files at the request of Zoe Pratt, perhaps to move money around."

"We were trying to prove her innocence," Zoe said.

Jack wished she'd remain quiet. They didn't

have many friends in the room, make that zero friends, and baiting the agent would only force him to take action against her.

And Jack. He didn't want to spend a night in jail, and be separated from Zoe. He struggled to come up with the right words to reduce the tension, convince the DEA of their honorable intentions.

"How well do you know them, Detective?" Trotter said.

"I met Zoe Pratt for the first time a few days ago after they brought her down off the mountain. Jack Monroe…" he hesitated "…I've known him for a few years."

"He illegally accessed bank accounts," Trotter said.

"That's unfortunate."

"Out of professional courtesy, I'll let this one pass once we clear him through a background check."

Jack sighed. There was no way Perry would burn a favor with the federal agency to free Jack. Instead of making eye contact with the detective, Jack studied Zoe. Her eyes flared as she looked at Detective Perry.

Out of the corner of his eye, Jack saw the detective glance in his direction.

"Let him go," Perry said. "He's one of the best search-and-rescue volunteers in Washington State."

Jack turned his attention to Perry, but he was focused on his phone. "They're sending teams into the mountains first thing tomorrow morning. They've narrowed down a new area of bunkers where someone could survive for days, maybe even weeks. Shannon Banks could have ended up there." He looked at the DEA agent. "You'll increase your odds of finding her if Jack is on the search team."

The next morning, as Zoe watched Jack pack up for the mission, she thanked God for his freedom. *Miracles do happen*, she thought as she remembered Detective Perry standing up for Jack, saying he was one of the best and discouraging the DEA agents from arresting him.

The federal agents ran background checks on both Zoe and Jack, and accepted the fact they were innocents caught up in a complex whirlwind of criminality.

Although the DEA agents had left last night, Zoe assumed they'd assigned an agent to the premises to keep an eye on things in case Shannon reached out to Zoe. She closed her eyes, fighting the image of Shannon being arrested at gunpoint if she were to randomly show up on her own.

Authorities seemed to be completely ignoring the fact Shan might be severely injured in the mountains. Zoe glanced out the window at the surrounding wilderness and sighed. She didn't care if Shan had gotten involved in something illegal, yet she also couldn't bring herself to believe it to be true.

All that mattered was getting her friend back alive.

Jack touched her shoulder. She looked up and was able to read his expression. He was offering comfort and strength.

"Keep praying for us," he said.

"I will."

He leaned forward and kissed her cheek. Her breath caught in her throat. It was a gentle kiss from a fascinating man.

"I will keep in touch via text message," Jack said.

"Thanks."

"You'll stay here, you won't leave the duplex?"

"Not even to get some French fries and ranch?"

He frowned with concern.

"I'm teasing. Don't worry. I'll stay here. If I'm desperate, I'll order room service. How long do you think…? Never mind, you probably have no idea."

"I'll be back as soon as the mission is complete." With a nod, Jack left.

She watched as Romeo jumped into the back seat of his SUV, Jack got behind the wheel and drove away, not looking back.

But she wanted him to look back. She wanted

him to acknowledge…what? That he cared about her, too?

Pressing her hand to her cheek, she realized she still felt the warmth of his lips there. How was it possible that during such an intense crisis Zoe had met a man she could very well be falling in love with?

Talk about a complicated situation: feelings amplified by physical danger, emotional worry and even grief. Yes, she was starting to grieve the potential loss of her friend. Even if she did return, Shannon may not be the person Zoe had known all those years ago.

Per Jack's request, Zoe sat at the kitchen table, interlaced her hands and prayed. She prayed for the search team's success, for their safety, for Shannon's return, and…for Jack, that no harm would come to him.

A sudden knock at the door startled her. She crossed the room and looked through the peephole.

Kelly stood on the other side of the door.

Zoe opened it and smiled. "Hi, Kelly."

"My shift starts in an hour. Do you want to grab something to eat at the restaurant?"

"I'm not supposed to leave the duplex. Why don't you come in and we'll order room service?"

"Okay." Kelly glanced over her shoulder. "You okay?"

"Sure, just paranoid I guess." Kelly joined her inside.

"That makes sense considering everything that happened yesterday."

"Walter fell into a coma last night."

"Oh no."

"Yeah, but not from the head injury. Apparently it was a drug overdose."

"Poor guy."

"Yeah, what a mess. This whole thing."

Trying to brighten Kelly's spirits, Zoe said, "I've got a good feeling about today's search."

"I like your optimism."

"Cheeseburgers okay?"

"Sure." Kelly pushed aside the curtain and peered outside. "There's a police cruiser in the lot."

"Probably keeping an eye on me."

Kelly glanced at her.

"Because I'm a target," Zoe said.

Kelly nodded and looked out the window.

Zoe ordered their meals and went into the kitchen to heat water for tea. *Tea calms the soul.* The memory of Jack's words comforted her.

A beep sounded from Kelly's phone. She glanced at it and spun around. "It's Shannon. She's here."

"What? Where?"

"Near the stables. She wants us to meet her." Kelly looked at Zoe. "She says she needs help."

Zoe grabbed her jacket and purse. She turned and hesitated. *Don't worry. I'll stay here.* She'd promised Jack she wouldn't leave.

"What's wrong?" Kelly said.

Zoe weighed her choices carefully. If she stayed here, she was turning her back on her best friend, ignoring her request for help.

She simply couldn't do it, not after everything that had happened.

She pulled out her phone to text Jack about where she was going.

"We've got to go now," Kelly said. "I saw the deputy walk away from his car, probably to get coffee or something. Hurry, so he won't see us leave."

Zoe pocketed her phone, slung her purse over her shoulder and followed Kelly to the door.

Kelly cracked it open and spied outside. "Let's go."

They left the duplex and Kelly shut the door, guiding Zoe quickly away, down the shoveled path past another duplex, then a quick right, so they'd be out of view of the police cruiser.

"How far is it?" Zoe asked.

"Not far."

"I hope she's okay. I mean, if she texted, then she's okay, right?" Zoe rambled.

A car suddenly pulled up. Zoe turned just as the original kidnapper got out and grabbed her.

"Stop!" she screamed. "Let me go!"

Kelly's eyes widened and she froze.

Before Zoe could *think* pepper spray, the guy applied a neck hold, pressing his arm against her throat and cutting off her ability to breathe or call out.

She struggled against him, swinging her arms. Her eyes watered.

Oh, why had they ditched the police surveillance?

Stars arced across her vision. She had to stay conscious, had to break free.

The pressure against her throat was too strong.

She struggled to breathe.

And lost consciousness.

THIRTEEN

Three teams had been assembled and assigned a specific search area. Jack and his team, consisting of Deputy Hauf and Sally Frick and her dog, Butch, hiked up the trail hoping to find evidence of Shannon Banks along the way. Even better, they hoped to find Shannon, either camped out or taking refuge in a bunker.

The only reason he'd joined this search was because there was a good chance he'd find Zoe's friend. Not only had the weather complied, but Command had gotten word that people had been seen in the area of the bunkers on the northern face of the mountain.

If it had been any other search for any other person, Jack would have stayed back to be with Zoe. However, this time he felt authorities had enough at stake that they wouldn't let her out of their sight. Even if they didn't consider Zoe a suspect, they knew her friendship with Shannon could be crucial in tracking down the missing woman.

Still, he hated leaving Zoe.

An odd turn of phrase. What would happen when this case was solved and they returned to their respective lives? He didn't want to think about that, wasn't sure how to process the thought.

It's not that complicated—you love her.

He stretched his neck and watched Romeo sniff

the ground up ahead. No, it wasn't possible to develop intense feelings like love in such a short period of time, was it? It surely wasn't logical.

Then again love wasn't a logical emotion.

Nor was it logical that he was slightly hurt that Zoe hadn't responded to his last text message, sent four minutes ago.

"Everything okay?" Sally asked.

He glanced at her in question.

"You've got this frown like you're trying to understand a foreign language."

"I'm okay, thanks."

"You're welcome." Her dog rushed back to her and tugged on her toggle. "What'd you find, Butch?"

Butch spun around and ran off. The human team members followed the dogs as they continued to lead them farther up the trail. A few minutes later Jack noticed the opening of a bunker. This could be it.

Deputy Hauf called it in and turned to Jack and Sally. "Keep your dogs back, and stay behind me."

Hauf drew his firearm and led the way. Although snow had fallen on and off these past few days, the trail was still manageable, thanks to determined hikers who would come up here regardless of weather conditions. Jack could understand why. Being out in nature tended to put everything into perspective, made problems and challenges seem smaller, more manageable.

He hoped he would have the chance to hike with Zoe once this was over.

Focus, Jack. Pay attention to your surroundings, to your K9 partner.

Romeo trotted in front of Jack. Sally and Butch were ahead of Romeo, and Deputy Hauf led the way. Jack didn't mind Hauf and Sally leading since they were both carrying firearms.

He found himself more concerned with his own welfare than usual.

Because of Zoe and their potential future together.

As they approached the bunker, Deputy Hauf put up his hand and snapped a flashlight off his belt. "Wait for me to give the all clear."

Romeo had other ideas and took off ahead of Deputy Hauf.

"Romeo, back," Jack said.

The dog stopped and turned to look at Jack. Jack tapped his thigh. The dog trotted to Jack's side, visibly frustrated.

Deputy Hauf entered the bunker.

As Jack and Sally waited, he noticed her unzip her jacket and rest her hand at her waist, where he assumed she kept her firearm.

Jack continued to scan the area for signs of anything unusual. Seconds stretched by slowly, as he worried about how he'd tell Zoe if or when they found Shannon's body. He wanted desperately for Zoe's friend to be alive. The thought of grief crushing Zoe's heart…

Pain ripped through him as surely as if he were feeling the potential grief.

He found himself silently praying, an odd, yet comforting feeling.

I'm new at this, God, but I could use Your support. Whatever we find, please help me find the words to comfort Zoe. Amen.

The pain in his chest seemed to soften a bit.

"Clear!" Deputy Hauf called.

The two K9 teams joined Deputy Hauf in the bunker. Jack was relieved that Shannon's body wasn't inside. The deputy was standing over an extinguished campfire. Jack knelt, took off his glove and touched the burned kindling. "Not warm."

Romeo burst into a round of barks. Deputy Hauf aimed his flashlight at the dog. Romeo was sniffing and pacing. Butch rushed up to him and barked. Jack spotted a scarf on the ground. With a brown stain.

"Blood," Jack said.

Deputy Hauf squatted, pulled a knife off his belt and used the tip to push the scarf aside. "This could belong to anyone."

"There's more over here," Sally said, aiming her flashlight into the corner where it appeared more articles of clothing were strewn on the ground. "More blood stains, like someone was trying to stop bleeding."

Jack pulled out his own flashlight and scanned the small area.

The beam illuminated a sparkle of silver against the dirt floor. "Deputy Hauf?" Jack motioned.

The deputy crossed the bunker and picked up a silver chain with the tip of his knife. A charm dangled from the end.

"It's a heart and a cross," Hauf said.

"It belongs to Shannon Banks," Jack said.

"How do you know?"

"She and Zoe have tattoos, same design."

"I'll call it in," Sally said, stepping out of the bunker.

It seemed that Shannon had been injured, but wasn't here now, which meant she'd hiked out on her own. That seemed hopeful.

"What's this?" Hauf pulled a tarp off a small mound to reveal plastic bags of a powdered substance. "This must be where they store the drugs."

Which meant, authorities would conclude Shannon's involvement in the drug ring since she was here, at the secret storage bunker.

"That doesn't necessarily mean—"

"Jack," Sally cut him off as she reentered the bunker. "They need you back ASAP. Zoe is gone."

The sound of men's voices awakened Zoe. She tentatively opened her eyes. She was on the floor, staring at a gray wall.

"What are we waiting for?"

"Confirmation he's got her."

Her? As in Shannon?

"Then what?"

"We end this thing. Let's go."

A few moments later there was the sound of a door clicking shut. Zoe sat up and looked around. She was in a one-room shed. A small lamp stood on a crate in the corner.

She spotted a man lying on the floor, his back to her. Rubbing her hands together, she realized the shed wasn't heated nor did it have windows.

She was a prisoner. Had they gotten Kelly, too?

The man coughed.

She tentatively crossed the shed. "Hello?"

He rolled over.

"Randy?" she said, recognizing him from the photo at Shan's house.

"I don't know you."

"I'm Zoe Pratt, a friend of Shannon's."

He nodded, but it seemed like he was out of it. The left side of his face was discolored with bruises, his pupils dilated, and he clutched his ribs with his arm.

"You're a DEA agent," she said.

He pinned her with dull green eyes.

"Agent Trotter told us about you, how you were assigned to make Shannon fall in love with you."

A slight chuckle escaped his lips and he winced,

closing his eyes. "Funny story… She would have made the better agent."

"What do you mean?"

When he opened his eyes again, Zoe knew instantly what he meant.

"You love her?" Zoe asked.

"Yeah, I fell for a drug dealer."

"I don't believe it."

"It's true. I lost my perspective."

"No, I mean the drug dealer part."

He nodded and closed his eyes.

Great. This guy loved Shannon, yet even he believed she was a drug dealer.

"Why are we here?" Zoe asked.

"Leverage. They've been trying to get Shannon to tell them where the drugs are," he hesitated, breathing slowly. "They think she's been stealing from them. But…"

"But?"

"I saw her…in the mountains."

"Is she okay?"

"Yeah. Acted like she had no idea what they were talking about, what they wanted."

"See, I knew it. She's not involved."

"She escaped." He winced as he shifted position. "Now that they have you, they've got the advantage. They think she'll do anything to save us." He looked at her, a sad smile easing across his lips. "The two people she loves."

"And if she doesn't?"

Randy shook his head and closed his eyes.

Jack returned to town in a state of…disassociation. He couldn't quite define any one feeling surging through him.

Anger? No. Frustration, yes. Panic, definitely. Disappointment, most definitely.

She'd gone against his wishes and left her safe accommodations.

Jack pulled up to the lodging and the first thing he noticed was the room service tray on the ground by the door. Why would she have ordered room service if she was going to flee?

He approached the duplex and the door swung open. Detective Perry scowled at him. "Okay, you know her better than anyone else in town. Where would she go?"

"Hello, Detective Perry." Jack entered.

"She's gone," Perry said. "Probably met up with Shannon. She's made so much money, she's probably paid for fake ID's and fled the jurisdiction."

"No, that's not Zoe. You don't know her."

"And you do?" Perry said. "Come on, Jack. You've known her for less than a week. I checked, she was having problems at work. They said she'd taken time off to reevaluate things. She comes up here, and she and Shannon cook up this kidnapping ploy, and then Zoe waits for Shannon to give her the green light to meet up."

"You're wrong."

"Great, well, if you know her so well, where'd she go?"

"I don't know."

"She didn't text you or call you? I mean, being that you're such good friends."

"I haven't heard from her." His gaze drifted across the room. He imagined her there, making tea, petting Romeo…smiling.

"You don't seem very upset," Detective Perry said.

"I'm upset."

"You know what this means?" Perry asked.

Jack looked at him.

"It means she's been manipulating you," Perry said.

Jack went to look out the window. *Where are you Zoe? Why did you go against my advice to stay put?*

The betrayal hurt worst of all.

Was it all a lie? Their intimate conversations? Discussions about faith? Her acceptance of his quirks and awkward demeanor? Had she been setting him up all along?

The thought tore through his insides. He hadn't felt this kind of pain when his ex-fiancée ended their relationship.

Detective Perry stepped up beside him. "Jack, I'm sorry."

Jack glanced at him, sensing Perry was apologizing for more than his harsh words.

"You're a smart guy. Help me out," Perry said. "Let's assume she isn't partners with Shannon."

Jack eyed him.

"I'm willing to take a leap of faith. If that's the case, why would she leave?"

"The only thing that would motivate her is the well-being of her best friend."

"Shannon."

"Yes."

"Then we're back to square one."

"Not necessarily. I can track her phone."

Perry quirked an eyebrow.

"I'm not a stalker."

Perry put up his hands. "No judgment."

Jack sat at the table and opened his laptop. "This program is better than the typical phone-tracking app. Give me a few minutes."

As Jack typed in the parameters, Detective Perry paced the living area.

"You're going to give yourself ulcerative colitis," Jack said.

"So I've been told. I hate being blindsided, first by the Feds, then by Zoe Pratt, the supposed victim."

So did Jack. He still wasn't sure what was going on, and the flood of emotional energy was so overpowering he chose numbness over emotion in order to process what was happening.

Zoe had left him.

Intentionally. There had been no sign of a struggle, no reports of a woman screaming. She'd left of her own volition.

Although, the food tray outside still bothered him.

As the program searched for Zoe's phone, Jack stood and went to the door.

"Where are you going?"

Jack opened the door, picked up the tray and brought it inside. "There are two plates here."

"Yeah?"

"She ordered food for two." He lifted the covers to reveal uneaten meals.

A ping rang from his laptop. He went to view it.

"She's not far away." Jack stood. "Are you notifying Agent Trotter?"

"They're in the mountains examining the bunker. I'll call a few of my deputies. Let's go."

Jack hesitated, surprised that the detective was including him in the search-and-retrieval mission.

Perry opened the door and looked at Jack. "Unless you don't want to."

"I'll follow you in my truck."

A key rumbled against a lock and Zoe dashed to her corner. She turned her back to the door and pretended to be asleep. The door shut with a click. She interlaced her fingers and prayed.

Jack, please find me.

That's when she realized if everyone thought Shan was a criminal, they might throw Zoe into that category as well, considering she'd mysteriously disappeared. She had to do something to let Jack know she was in trouble.

"They're both asleep," a man said.

He must be on the phone. But what would he do when the call ended?

She reached for her Holy Spirit charm to calm herself. As her fingers touched the smooth silver dove, the answer became clear.

"It's better if we do it up there anyway. Easier to dispose of the bodies."

The bodies? As in dead bodies? Her heart raced.

A sudden needle prick at the base of her neck made her yelp.

She swung her arm to push the guy away.

"Keep still."

Suddenly he was yanked back. Randy was trying to defend her, get her free. As the men struggled, she scanned the small shed and spotted a footstool.

The kidnapper shoved Randy against the wall.

Zoe swung the footstool at the kidnapper's head. He spun around and grabbed Zoe's wrist. It was the guy who attacked her on the mountain and took Shannon. A shudder ran down her spine.

"Enough," he said. "Or I'll kill you both right here."

He shoved her aside and she stumbled, falling

on the dirt floor of the shed. As she looked up, it felt like she was watching a movie, like she wasn't the one in the shed being brutalized.

The drug. It must already be taking effect.

"Now let's go," he said, pulling Randy up. "You, too."

She knew he was talking to her, but her mind felt soggy.

He grabbed her arm.

She wrapped her fingers around her necklace, yanked hard and dropped it by her side.

Find this, Jack. Find my necklace and come save me.

One last time.

FOURTEEN

Jack tracked Zoe's phone to a shed on the far perimeter of the resort property. Detective Perry contacted the resort manager, Curt, to notify him they needed access. Curt gladly gave Detective Perry the key.

Two sheriff's deputies, two DEA agents, Detective Perry and Jack surrounded the small shed. Perry led the team. He approached the door. Inserted the key and turned the lock. With a nod to his team, he swung the door open. "Police!"

His deputies followed him inside the shed.

A few long seconds of painstaking silence passed, then—

"Clear!"

Jack hurried into the shed behind DEA agents. And saw a woman on the ground wearing a knit cap. "Zoe?"

He wasn't even sure if he'd said her name aloud. His heart clenched.

Detective Perry put out his hand for everyone to stay back. The two deputies, Ortman and Hauf, made room for Jack. Detective Perry gently rolled the female over.

It was Shannon's friend, Kelly.

Relief warred with panic in Jack's chest. It wasn't Zoe, which was good, but then where was she?

"Ma'am, can you hear me?" Detective Perry asked.

Jack vaguely sensed the other DEA agents searching the shed.

"I…what?" she said.

"Detective?" one of the DEA agents said, as he picked up a cell phone.

Zoe's phone.

"Ma'am, are you okay?" Perry said.

"Her name is Kelly," Jack offered.

"Kelly, can you hear me?" Perry said.

"I…yes."

"What happened?"

"Zoe… Shannon…"

"They were here?"

Kelly nodded. "It's cold." She wrapped her arms around herself and started shivering.

"Find me a blanket," Perry said. One of his deputies rushed out of the shed.

"You saw Shannon Banks?" Perry redirected to Kelly.

"Yes. She and Zoe left."

"Do you know where they went?"

Deputy Hauf returned with a blanket and Perry wrapped it around Kelly's body.

"Thank you," she said.

"Did they say where they were going?"

"Canada."

Perry nodded at the DEA agents. "Notify Trotter so you can intercept them at the border. We need an ambulance."

"On its way," Deputy Hauf said from the doorway.

Detective Perry helped Kelly sit up. He glanced over his shoulder at Jack. "Sorry."

Jack nodded but didn't respond. What could he say? That yes, he was, in fact a complete fool? He shook his head and glanced down.

That's when he saw it. A flash of silver on the floor. He crouched and picked it up.

Zoe's silver dove charm. She never would have left it behind, not intentionally.

"You find something?" Perry said.

Jack glanced sideways and noticed Kelly watching him with an odd expression. Zoe would know what it meant. As Jack struggled to interpret its meaning, the blanket slipped off her shoulder.

Exposing a patch on her black hoodie. Of a bald eagle.

In a flash, things started to click in Jack's head.

If it had been Kelly giving drugs to Jeanie… and perhaps to Walter…

Kelly was the drug dealer, not Shannon.

Anything that came out of Kelly's mouth was a lie; the story about Zoe and Shannon heading to Canada meant as a diversion. But he needed to play along. He didn't want Kelly informing her cohorts that they'd been exposed.

Jack nodded at Detective Perry. "They'll call

off the search for Shannon Banks since she's on her way to Canada. Are you done with me?"

Perry studied him with a curious expression. "Sure. Thanks for your help."

"You're welcome." He exited the shed and walked toward his truck.

Curt, the resort manager, pulled up in a company vehicle. "Did you find them?"

"Kelly, yes. But not Zoe or Shannon."

"How is she?"

"She'll be okay," Jack said, assuming as much since she was involved in this criminal activity.

"Will Search and Rescue—"

"They'll most likely call off the search since Miss Banks and Miss Pratt are said to be heading to Canada."

Curt sighed. "So, the threat is over."

Not hardly.

With a nod, Jack got in his truck and considered his options. Time was of the essence. The real criminals, of which Kelly was one, were sending authorities north to Canada, which meant Zoe and Shannon were not heading north.

He took a deep breath and decided to flip the entire hypothesis on its head.

If Shannon was the victim...

If Shannon, as the DEA claimed, was transporting product across the border but didn't know the contents of her transport... But someone else did—Kelly—and she started to skim off the top...

Everything started to make sense.

If the criminals thought Shannon was stealing, they'd demand their product be returned. If she pleaded ignorance, because she had no idea what they were talking about, they'd find another way to pressure her into returning the stolen product, like threatening someone she cared about…

That's why they'd been after Zoe from day one. Not because she could identify the kidnapper, but because they could use Zoe as leverage against Shannon.

Jack and Romeo had to find Zoe, and they had no time to spare. They couldn't do it alone so he sent two text messages, one to Sally Frick and the other to Detective Perry.

"This could be dangerous, buddy," he said to his dog who sat patiently in the back seat.

Jack pulled away to convince anyone who was watching him that he was leaving, giving up.

But he'd never give up on Zoe.

Hiking.

Zoe was hiking again. Up into the mountains.

The last time she went hiking, she'd been with…

"Shannon?" she said, as she put one foot in front of the other.

"She's meeting us up ahead," a man's voice said.

Zoe felt like she was floating, her boots light,

her mind cushioned by a purple cloud of happiness. Yes, she was very happy, ecstatic because she was going to see Shannon.

Her friend had been lost for days. Search-and-rescue teams had scoured the mountain.

"Romeo?" she said, looking for Jack's dog. Jack and Romeo must have found Shannon and were waiting for Zoe.

Someone nudged her from behind, she stumbled and nearly fell onto the snowy trail. She giggled, thinking how silly she would have looked falling down like a child.

She glanced over her shoulder and saw a large man wearing a ski mask pulling up another man who had fallen.

"Up!" the big guy shouted.

The man struggling to stand had a kind, furry face and bloodshot eyes. Zoe helped him up. "Upsy-daisy." She looked at the guy with the ski mask. "Why are you being so mean?"

"We've got to get to Shannon before the weather breaks."

"Oh, okay." She turned to the man who'd fallen, and remembered who he was—Shan's boyfriend, Randy. "Didn't you hear him? Shan's waiting for us. Come, come." Zoe encouraged Randy forward.

She hadn't a clue where they were going, but as long as Shannon would be there, it didn't matter.

She wasn't sure how much time had passed when she spotted the fire lookout. Shannon had mentioned seeing God's beauty from there. This had to be the place where she would meet Zoe and Randy. Zoe could hardly contain herself. She'd been so worried about her friend...

...Because why again?

Because she'd gone missing. And then authorities were saying horrible things about Shan, things Zoe refused to believe.

Zoe approached the last rocky bit of trail.

Her ankle turned and she lost her balance, but Randy grabbed her from behind.

"Thank you," she said, stepping onto the porch surrounding the lookout. She went around to an open door.

"Shannon?" She stepped inside.

Shannon, who sat in the corner of the one room structure looked up. "Zoe?"

Zoe rushed to her friend and they embraced. "Randy's here, too."

"Randy?"

"Isn't it great?" Zoe said.

"What's going on?" Shannon said to someone behind Zoe.

Zoe turned and spotted a man she recognized. A police officer.

"Oh, Sergeant Peterson, thank you for finding my friend," Zoe said.

Randy stumbled and fell onto the floor. Shannon went to his side. "Are you okay?"

The big man stepped into the lookout.

Shannon pulled Randy away and clung to him.

"Shannon?" Zoe said.

"Zoe, get out of here!" Shannon cried.

Zoe glanced at the big guy and then at Sergeant Peterson. "It's okay, Shannon. Sergeant Peterson is here. He'll protect us."

The sergeant tapped his fingers against his belt.

"How could I have been so stupid?" Shannon said.

"What do you mean?" Zoe said.

The big guy grabbed Randy's arm to pull him away from Shannon.

"No!" Shannon cried.

"Tell us where it is, or I'll slice him up right here in front of you."

"Stop," Sergeant Peterson said.

Zoe sighed with relief.

"We're waiting on orders," the sergeant said.

"You don't need orders to arrest a bad guy," Zoe offered.

The sergeant looked at her.

"Use your gun, show him your badge." Zoe motioned with her hands.

"Oh, Zoe," Shannon said softly.

"What?"

"He *is* one of the bad guys."

Zoe was confused. She looked at Shannon, then at the sergeant. Zoe couldn't process what it was all about, but she knew one thing for sure. She wished Jack were here.

The sound of footsteps echoed against the wooden platform. Curt, the resort manager, stepped inside.

"Curt?" Shannon said.

"Yes, Shannon, it's me, the man you've been betraying for the past three months."

"I don't know what—"

"Stop!" Curt stepped closer to Shannon. "Did you honestly think you could steal from me and I wouldn't notice? Do I seem that stupid?"

"Steal what? Specialty linens?"

Curt burst out laughing. The other two men stood there, stone-faced. Zoe hugged herself. Something terrible was happening.

"You have my drugs and I want them back," he said.

"I didn't take your drugs. I didn't even know I was transporting drugs."

"Police found a stash in a bunker on the north face of the mountain," Sergeant Peterson said to no one in particular.

"Tell me you didn't store my drugs in a damp bunker," Curt said to Shannon.

"I didn't take and never had your drugs."

"No?" Curt nodded at the big guy.

He crossed the small space toward Zoe and grabbed her arm.

"No, don't!" Shannon charged and he back-handed her.

"You jerk!" Zoe bit the big guy's hand that

clung to her arm. He tossed her aside and she hit the floor, hard.

As she lay there, head throbbing, she decided to pray: for her life, for Shannon's and Randy's life. For Jack to come find her.

The sound of a dog barking gave her hope. Romeo.

"Did you hear that?" Sergeant Peterson said.

To mask the sound of Romeo barking, Zoe started singing "Amazing Grace," rather loudly.

"Where are the drugs!" Curt shouted at Shannon.

"'…to save a wretch like me…'" Zoe sang.

"No! Leave Randy alone!" Shan shouted.

"'… Was blind but now I see…'"

"There's someone out there," the big guy said.

"Check it out," Curt ordered, then turned and started kicking Randy.

"She doesn't care about the boyfriend. She cares about this one." Sergeant Peterson grabbed Zoe.

She yelped and stopped singing.

Romeo's barking echoed across the mountain range.

Sergeant Peterson released Zoe and went to the window.

The barking continued.

He withdrew his firearm from his holster and cracked open a window.

"Nooo!" Zoe charged him.

The gun went off.

The sergeant shoved her aside and aimed his weapon at her.

A gunshot rang out. Zoe automatically dropped to the wood floor and pinched her eyes shut. It didn't hurt. Nothing hurt. How was that possible? She hugged herself and rocked back and forth.

"Freeze!"

She cracked open her eyes…

And saw Sergeant Peterson sprawled on the floor in front of her. Detective Perry stood in the doorway aiming his weapon.

What just happened?

Perry entered the lookout and someone pushed around him to get to Zoe.

Jack. He rushed to her and pulled her against this chest.

"You found me," she said.

"Romeo found you."

"Is he okay?"

"Romeo, right here!"

The dog darted into the lookout and rushed up to Zoe. "Help her," Jack said.

Romeo nuzzled Zoe's leg and licked her hand.

"Oh, Romeo, you're my hero." She glanced up into Jack's rich blue eyes. "You, too, Jack. I love you both."

FIFTEEN

As they sat in the conference room at the sheriff's office, Zoe wondered why Jack wasn't making eye contact. He'd been acting more aloof than usual since they'd returned to town. Was that it? In his mind, once the case was over, was their relationship over, too?

Or was he embarrassed that she'd professed to love him back at the lookout? She couldn't stop herself. She'd been under the influence of the drugs they'd given her and had completely lost her filter.

The truth was she *did* love Jack or was starting to love him or… Whatever, it didn't matter anyway.

"I made good money transporting supplies for the resort, extra money I donated to the community center youth programs," Shannon said. "I had no idea I was smuggling drugs." She shuddered. "So I was like a mule or something?"

"Yes, ma'am," Agent Trotter said. "Curt Underwood was the leader of this operation, with support from Sergeant Peterson."

Detective Perry clenched his jaw.

"I still can't believe it," Shannon said. "I volunteered with him at Angie's Youth Club. That's why I called him, why I trusted him above everyone else."

"We all trusted him," Detective Perry said.

"How did he get involved in this?" Zoe said.

"His son is seriously ill and needed treatment at Children's Hospital," Agent Trotter said. "Peterson ran out of money. Curt found out and made him an offer. Peterson felt he had no choice."

"That's so sad," Zoe said. "So that's why Curt's men always knew where I was, because Sergeant Peterson told them?"

"That and because Kelly was tracking your phone. She'd also cloned Shannon's."

"That's how she was able to send text messages that looked like they were coming from Shannon," Jack said, leaning back in his chair.

"Once product started disappearing from your shipments, Curt hired Vic Jones to kidnap you, threaten you and convince you to turn it over," Trotter said to Shannon. "But you didn't, so they came after the people you cared about."

"Randy and Zoe," Shannon said softly.

"I'm okay," Zoe said, glancing at Jack.

"He also had a second man working for him, the one who broke into Shannon's house, and was killed trying to break out of jail. We suspect Curt was the other man at the scene."

"But why blow up my house?" Shannon asked.

"To convince authorities you were involved with a violent drug cartel," Trotter said. "Curt sent Kelly Washburn to cut the gas line and leave a candle burning, which set off the explosion. Kelly was who you saw fleeing the scene wearing a jacket similar to Shannon's. Everything she did, she did with the intention of making it look like Shannon was a criminal."

Shannon shook her head. "Why would she get involved in this? I mean, she didn't have a sick child or anything."

"Some people don't need a noble motivation. They just like money," Trotter said. "She knew Curt was having you smuggle product against your knowledge and decided the fact you two look similar could work in her favor. She was skimming off your shipments so she looked clean to her boss. Then, pretending to be you, she'd sell product to customers. She made a nice chunk of change."

"That's why Jeanie thought I was selling her drugs. Because Kelly was pretending to be me," Shannon said. "And to think I kicked her out of the club because she kept demanding I get her more stuff. I had no idea what she was talking about and she became hysterical."

"What about Jeanie?" Zoe asked.

"She's home and safe with her father," Detective Perry said. "If you want to press charges—"

"We don't." Zoe glanced at Jack, but he was still avoiding eye contact.

"Not only had Kelly been selling to kids at the community center, but she also took the lead on throwing us off course during the investigation,"

Agent Trotter said, addressing Shannon. "She left the bloodstained clothes in the bunker to convince us you were too injured to survive, and she left drugs there as evidence against you."

"What about the woman who died in the mountains?" Zoe asked.

"A customer of Kelly's," Trotter said. "The young woman had Shannon's name written on a piece of paper, but it had the number for a burner phone probably belonging to Kelly."

"Kelly Washburn did everything in her power to convince authorities you were the mastermind of this drug operation," Perry said to Shannon.

Shan looked at Zoe. "Did you think…?"

"She didn't," Jack said.

Everyone in the room turned to him.

"Not for one minute did she believe you could be capable of smuggling or dealing drugs," Jack reiterated. "She used your journal to try to prove your innocence. That's how much she believed in you."

Zoe offered a smile. He still wouldn't look at her.

"Shannon, why didn't you notify police sooner when you found out what was going on?" Agent Trotter said.

"I didn't find out until after I'd been kidnapped. The kidnapper kept demanding to know where *it* was. I had no idea what he was talking about. Even after Randy told me not to trust anyone, I called the one person I thought was solid, Sergeant Peterson. That blew up in my face."

"You couldn't have known, honey," Zoe said.

"No, but I should have," Detective Perry said. "My apologies, Shannon."

"Thank you. I'm glad everyone's okay." She glanced around the table.

Zoe noticed Randy wouldn't make eye contact with Shannon either.

"I'm still amazed you survived out there for so long," Zoe said.

"Me, too. I actually escaped that first day, but he caught me again and kept me hidden in a bunker on the east side of the mountain. Then Randy found me and helped me escape the second time. Randy?"

He finally looked up.

"Thank you."

He nodded, and lowered his gaze.

Shannon turned to Zoe. "I'm sorry you got dragged into all of this."

"Hey, it's not your fault. Besides, I met some exceptional people while in town." She cast a quick glance at Jack, who was studying his phone.

Her heart sank. Case over; relationship over.

"We'll need both of you to testify against Curt Underwood and his men," Trotter said.

"Of course," Shannon said.

"Why do you need Zoe?" Jack said.

Again, everyone looked at him.

"She's been in enough danger for one lifetime," Jack offered.

"The players have all been arrested. There's no one left to pose a threat to her," Agent Trotter said.

Jack nodded but didn't look satisfied with the answer.

Okay, so he wouldn't even look at Zoe, but he was worried about her safety? How...inconsistent.

They wrapped up the meeting and Shannon turned to Zoe. "I'll be right back."

Shan followed Randy outside to talk to him. Zoe watched the intense exchange from the doorway.

"Are you okay?" Jack asked, approaching her.

She turned to him, trying to read his shuttered expression.

"Sure," she said.

"You don't sound so sure of your sure."

He was joking with her?

"I'm still processing it all," she said.

"It can take weeks or even months to recover from a trauma such as the one you've experienced this past week. Wait, why am I telling you this? You're the counselor."

She nodded. "That's right, I am." Yet she had no idea how to communicate with the man standing in front of her.

"I've heard good things about something called EMDR for trauma victims," Jack said.

"I'm familiar."

"You could also—"

"It's you, Jack. You're what's upsetting me right now."

"Okay, I'll leave." He turned and she grabbed his arm.

"No, not you, the person. It's your behavior."

"Did I say something rude again?"

"No, that's the point. You're not saying anything. You can barely look at me."

"I can't help it. I'm going to miss you."

"We can remedy that. We can—"

"No, we can't."

"See, I'm confused. I thought you felt—"

"I do. I feel a lot…about you. Which is why this can't happen."

"For a smart guy you're making absolutely no sense here, Jack."

"I can't give you what you need."

"And what's that?" She crossed her arms over her chest, wondering where this was going.

"I will never be able to fulfill your needs emotionally, so instead, I will remove myself from your life so you can find someone who can. It was…" he hesitated "…amazing, knowing you, Zoe Pratt, spending time with you, even under the circumstances."

He leaned forward and kissed her cheek. Again.

She was stunned. Flummoxed. Nonplussed.

This incredible man was worried about her emotional needs, and since he believed he fell short, he would simply remove himself from her life. He cared about her that much.

She started to call after him but wasn't sure what to say.

Shannon approached and put her arm around Zoe. "You were busy while I was kidnapped and held hostage in the mountains," she said.

"He doesn't think he's worthy of me."

"He's not. No one is." Shannon gave Zoe a squeeze.

"That's not true." She glanced at Shannon. "If anyone's worthy, it's a guy like Jack."

"Let's go decompress at the hotel and figure out what to do about our guy trouble."

Back to work. Back to normal.

Jack had a hard time sitting still, focusing. He paced to the window overlooking Puget Sound.

"I'm not sure about Quantum Enterprises. There's something about the CEO that makes me think they'd be difficult to work with," Heather, Jack's assistant, said.

Everything struck him as difficult lately.

"I could set up an introductory meeting if you want to check it out for yourself?"

"No, I trust your judgment." Besides he didn't have the bandwidth to sign on with difficult clients. He wasn't sure what he had the energy for these days.

"Okay," Heather said. "Unicom Properties

wants to know when you'll be testing their system."

He turned to Heather. "If I tell them, then they'll try to prepare. That defeats the purpose of my service."

"Good point."

Jack's phone vibrated. He glanced at a text from Zoe. He looked away. Glanced back at the phone.

"SAR?" Heather asked.

"What?"

"You keep looking at your phone. Did you get a search-and-rescue alert?"

"No. It's a female."

"O-kay," she chuckled.

"I don't understand females."

"Want me to…?" She motioned.

He handed her his phone. She read aloud, "'I have never felt so cherished, understood or safe with a man.'" Heather looked up. "What's the confusion?"

"I don't understand what that means."

"Uh…boss? I think it means she loves you."

He paced to his bookshelves and analyzed the binding on a hardcover edition of a coding textbook.

Love? Even after he'd told her he was broken, that he couldn't give her everything she needed?

The phone pinged with another text. He turned to Heather. "Read it, please."

"She's asking you to meet her at Serenity Lake

Overlook tomorrow." She stood. "You've only got one meeting tomorrow. I'll handle it. I'll put off the Principality meet and greet until next week and tell Unicom March 1."

"Why March 1?"

"To throw them off track so they won't be prepared."

"But—"

"Nothing is more important than love, boss." She handed him back his phone. "Even a man as brilliant as you must know that."

Zoe checked her phone. 12:17 p.m.

He wasn't coming.

She paced the area overlooking Serenity Lake. Jack knew where to find her, both from her text and the fact he was probably still tracking her phone location.

Which meant he'd chosen not to come.

Well, she never would have forgiven herself if she hadn't tried, hadn't reached out one last time.

She accepted the fact you couldn't fix another person, couldn't give them the confidence they needed or make them feel something they didn't.

Yet Jack felt love for Zoe. He'd admitted as much. He just didn't believe himself good enough to make her happy.

"Oh, Jack," she said softly. Zoe believed in her heart that he was exactly the type of man who would be a good life partner. He was honest to a fault, caring of others and had a high moral compass. A wonderful combination.

He'd even seemed to open his heart to God during the short time they'd spent together.

Was she crazy for feeling this way? *No*, she reminded herself, *you can't control your feelings, you have to name them and embrace them*.

She had fallen in love with Jack Monroe.

Crossing her arms over her chest, she gazed out across the gorgeous aquamarine lake below. It was beautiful here. Even after all the trauma of the past week, beauty ruled over darkness.

If she left town in a few days with a wounded heart, she'd still focus on the things she'd learned, like the fact it was okay to rely on another person for help. She didn't have to do everything on her own.

She had relied on Jack.

A text vibrated and she glanced at her phone, hopeful. It was Shannon, checking in. Zoe was optimistic for her friend since Shannon and Randy had been spending time together. Randy had begged for Shannon's forgiveness, both for suspecting her of being involved in the drug scheme and for having to lie to her about his motivations. He said he loved her so much he'd consider quitting the DEA to be with her.

Now that was true love.

Zoe responded to Shan that Jack was a no-show, and pocketed her phone. She decided to say one last prayer of surrender. Interlacing her fingers and closing her eyes, she said, "Dear Lord, I know I've done my best to open his heart, to make him feel safe and loved. If it's not meant to be, then I surrender my pain to You and pray that You help Jack find peace, love and happiness. Amen."

She took a few slow, deep breaths.

The sound of a barking dog filled her heart with joy. She turned just as Romeo raced up to her. She dropped to her knees and embraced him.

As she buried her face into his fur, she thanked God for what she hoped was about to happen.

Jack joined her and she stood, offering a smile. "You're eighteen minutes late."

"Nineteen actually. Please forgive me. There was an accident in Darrington and I tried texting but couldn't get service in the pass."

He reached out and took her hand. The warmth shot clear up to her heart.

"I'm glad you waited," he said.

"Me, too." She squeezed his hand and gazed across the lake, marveling at the beauty below. "I like it here."

"It's the view," Jack said, studying her. He offered a smile and pulled her into a hug. "Is this okay?"

"It's perfect."

"Perfect. As good as it is possible to be." He broke the hug and looked directly into her eyes.

"Your text… I wasn't sure… I mean, after what I said about not being able to make you happy."

"Look at my face." She cracked a wide smile. "This is my happy face, and it's how I feel when I'm with you."

"Oh, good. I mean my assistant interpreted the text—"

"My text needed an interpreter? Wow, I'm honored."

He actually smiled, indicating he understood she was joking around.

"I needed her assistance because I wanted to confirm I wasn't misreading things," he said.

"You weren't."

"That's a first."

She chuckled and searched his eyes. "What about your plan to sell your company and go on adventures? I'll be honest, Jack, I'm not the type to pick up and leave for months at a time."

"I think…" he offered a half grin "…this adventure will be better."

He kissed her, a warm kiss filled with promise, devotion and love.

* * * * *

Look for more books from Hope White coming soon from Love Inspired Suspense!

Dear Reader,

Sometimes it's a struggle to find hope when confronted with stressful situations. Yet hope and faith are so important to help us stay on the path of grace.

Zoe Pratt clings to hope that her friend is both safe and that she hasn't gotten mired in criminal activity. Through faith and prayer, Zoe remains strong and realizes that even if her friend has made poor choices, Zoe will forgive her because she—and God—love her unconditionally.

Hope is a mystery to Jack Monroe since his own hope was extinguished as a child, and again as a young man. Yet by watching Zoe's dedication to hope, something is rekindled in his heart. Jack admires her devotion and realizes it might be worth opening his heart to God, friendship and something more.

Jack and Zoe learn from each other by appreciating their differences and accepting each other for who they are, their flaws as well as their strengths. By the end of this story, they find that unconditional love opens the door to remarkable things, including love and grace.

Peace,
Hope White

Get 4 FREE REWARDS!

We'll send you 2 FREE Books <u>plus</u> 2 FREE Mystery Gifts.

Love Inspired books feature uplifting stories where faith helps guide you through life's challenges and discover the promise of a new beginning.

FREE Value Over $20

COMING NEXT MONTH FROM
Love Inspired Suspense

Available March 3, 2020

FUGITIVE TRAIL
K-9 Mountain Guardians • by Elizabeth Goddard

When an escaped convict vows revenge on Deputy Sierra Young, former coworker turned PI Bryce Elliott is determined to protect her. But can Bryce, Sierra and her search-and-rescue K-9, Samson, track the fugitive before he succeeds in taking their lives?

FALSELY ACCUSED
FBI: Special Crimes Unit • by Shirlee McCoy

Framed for her foster brother's murder, FBI special agent Wren Santino must clear her name—but someone's dead set on stopping her from finding the truth. Now with help from her childhood friend Titus Anderson, unraveling a conspiracy may be the only way to survive.

AMISH COUNTRY MURDER
by Mary Alford

As the sole woman to escape the Dead of Night Killer, Catherine Fisher's the key to catching him—if he doesn't kill her first. But with her memory missing and all clues indicating the serial killer targeted her for very personal reasons, it'll take everything FBI agent Sutter Brenneman has to keep her safe.

MOUNTAIN CAPTIVE
by Sharon Dunn

Private investigator Jude Trainor won't give up on finding a kidnapped little girl—even when the suspect runs him off a mountain road and sends bullets his way. But when Lacey Conrad rescues Jude on her snowmobile, can they outlast a snowstorm *and* a person who wants them dead?

STOLEN SECRETS
by Sherri Shackelford

After she discovers someone's been impersonating her to steal classified technology secrets, Lucy Sutton has to figure out who's behind it. National Security Agency employee Jordan Harris is the only person she trusts. But capturing the culprit is an even deadlier task than they expected.

KILLER HARVEST
by Tanya Stowe

With her boss murdered, Sassa Nilsson's the last person who can save the world's crops from a lethal plant pathogen. But with criminals willing to kill Sassa to get the formula for the virus, can border patrol agent Jared De Luca shield her?

ReaderService.com has a new look!

We have refreshed our website and
we want to share our new look with you.
Head over to ReaderService.com
and check it out!

On ReaderService.com, you can:

- Try 2 free books from any series
- Access risk-free special offers
- View your account history & manage payments
- Browse the latest Bonus Bucks catalog

RS19